# DEAD AHEAD

## GRAVE TALKER SERIES BOOK FIVE
### ANNIE ANDERSON

DEAD AHEAD

*Arcane Souls World*

*Grave Talker Book 5*

*International Bestselling Author*

Annie Anderson

Edited by Angela Sanders

Cover Design by Tattered Quill Designs

www.annieande.com

# BOOKS BY ANNIE ANDERSON

## THE ARCANE SOULS WORLD

### GRAVE TALKER SERIES

*Dead to Me*

*Dead & Gone*

*Dead Calm*

*Dead Shift*

*Dead Ahead*

*Dead Wrong*

### SOUL READER SERIES

*Night Watch*

*Death Watch*

*Grave Watch*

### THE WRONG WITCH SERIES

*Spells & Slip-ups*

# THE ETHEREAL WORLD

## PHOENIX RISING SERIES

*(Formerly the Ashes to Ashes Series)*

*Flame Kissed*

*Death Kissed*

*Fate Kissed*

*Shade Kissed*

*Sight Kissed*

## ROGUE ETHEREAL SERIES

*Woman of Blood & Bone*

*Daughter of Souls & Silence*

*Lady of Madness & Moonlight*

*Sister of Embers & Echoes*

*Priestess of Storms & Stone*

*Queen of Fate & Fire*

# TRIGGER WARNING

This book may contain triggers for sensitive readers.
Due to the mature subject matter, it is recommended for
readers ages 18 and older.

I was going to punch a god right in the face.

Sure, he was the actual God of Torment, dread, and fear. Okay, so he probably didn't deserve it. But I would sock him right in the mouth...

Just as soon as I got the nerve.

"Now, that's just rude," Deimos muttered, straightening the tie of his impossibly crisp suit as he stared me down.

I was a tall woman at nearly six feet, but this dude made me feel teeny—especially when he fixed his scarred, mismatched gaze on me. This also had me wondering what could possibly cut a god bad enough to leave a scar like that. The porch of the Knoxville Warden house never seemed so small, though it wasn't like I'd actually inspected the place before now.

"I came here to have a civil discussion," he tutted, as if I were a naughty puppy that had just piddled on his rug, "and all you can think of is violence."

*Yep. Definitely going to punch a god in the face.*

It was one thing to come here—after the absolute catastrophe of the last twenty-four hours, I could get that—but to imply he was here for anything other than to beg for my fucking forgiveness for what his son had done to me, well...

"A civil discussion? A *civil discussion?*" The laugh that came out of my mouth made me sound cracked even to my own ears. "Maybe the reason all I want to do is hit something is because *your son* wormed his way inside my skull," I seethed, roughly tapping my temple as I stepped forward. "*And* he killed two people with *my* hands. Maybe it's because he didn't exactly ask permission first before he wore me like a skin suit while he got himself free. Maybe it's because I have been violated beyond measure after losing half my damn family. Really, the possibilities are endless as to why violence is on the menu."

Another unhinged giggle popped free of my mouth, which had Deimos shuffling backward a pace or two.

Or five.

"You freed my son—"

"I didn't free shit," I spat, following him down the

steps and across the ribbon of pavement that bisected the front yard. "Did you miss the part where he wore me without consent? Add to that, Azrael locked me inside my own mind, so I couldn't even shove *your son* out, either. Oh, no. You aren't pinning this shit on me."

And if it was possible that I *may* have yelled that at a god while slowly stalking him across the grass, well, then, so be it. I'd had a rough couple of days, compounded by the worst month ever, on top of a *spectacularly* shitty year. Yelling should be allowed.

Deimos stilled his feet and rolled his head on his neck, the faint crack of the joints popping making me smirk. I used to do the same thing to Mariana when I wanted to make her cringe. It was one thing to pop your fingers, but the neck? Gave her the creeps every time. A little smile lifted the edge of the god's lips, and I had to roll my eyes.

The dick had done it on purpose. But that wouldn't make me think he was on my side. I didn't trust him any more than I did his son, and considering the involuntary possession and murder bit? Yeah, that was not at all.

"As I was saying," He paused, waiting for me to interrupt, and when I didn't, he continued, "you freed my son. I would like you to find hi—"

"No." I didn't even have to think about it or let him finish that sentence. There was no way on this green earth—or any other planet for that matter—that I would willfully go and seek out the demon that had just put blood on my hands.

No. Way.

A faint rumbling came from Deimos' throat that caused all the little hairs on my arms to stand on end. To call it a growl would be too infantile, and to call it a bark would be too lewd. This was something altogether different and terrifying enough that I took two steps back and shut all the way up.

"I do not enjoy being interrupted, child—especially by the whelp responsible for setting him free."

*The fuck I did.*

"I did *not* set Aemon free," I stupidly argued, my mouth running away from me. No matter how true it was, Deimos didn't seem to like taking criticism.

*Not that it stopped me.*

"That bitchy agent who tried to kill me made the deal that let him out of that box. You want the person responsible? Go find her. I'm sure her ghost is running around here somewhere if she's not in Hell already." I paused, considering something for the first time. "And why was he in a coffin in the first place? Who puts an easily crackable wooden box on Earth with a Prince of Hell inside? Don't you have a perfectly good torture chamber in your own backyard? Seems like poor planning to me."

To say that Deimos did not appreciate me pointing these things out, was a bit of an understatement. He stalked forward, the color of both irises changing from their respective pale blue and hazel to a matching blood-red that only seemed to highlight the rather intimidating scar that ran through his left eye.

"Why he was there is no concern of yours. Neither is the reason I'm calling you to this task. Your concern is finding my son. Or else."

And that's about when I started the deranged giggling again. "Or what? You'll kill me? I bet not since my sister is the new Angel of Death. Take me to Hell? It would probably be a vacation. Threaten me and mine? Better men than you have tried and failed. So, tell me—what is your 'or else'?"

Did I care that I had a literal god on my front walk, bitching about something I had no control over? Maybe. But I wasn't going to be threatened, used, or abused. Not by this god and not by his son.

Not ever again.

"Do it—whatever it is. Go ahead. If I haven't cracked yet, whatever you have up your sleeve may as well be a fucking party."

I doubted Deimos had ever met a woman as close to

the end of her rope as I was because his tactics changed immediately. His eyes lost their menacing glow and his shoulders relaxed. His jaw unclenched, and the hands that had been balled into fists, straightened. And while I could suppose that all this had the potential to be comforting to some, every single movement put me on red alert and wishing I had a god-killing bullet or a Deimos-sized cage or *something*.

"Aemon is not a demon you want to be running around this realm. If you can't see that, if you do not desire him to be caught and locked away immediately, well, then I cannot help you."

Groaning, my whole body seemed to wither as the sound escaped my lungs. "You probably should have led with that, but I still can't help *you*."

I held up a hand, cutting off whatever rebuttal was on his lips next. I still remembered the hot pulse of power coursing through my body as Aemon left it, the way that agent's face went slack as the life drained out of her after he'd slit her throat with my hands. The crushing blows to Bishop's body as he tried and failed to stop the demon. The wicked burn that filled my whole body as he "healed" me.

I had enough on my plate.

"I can't. This is above my pay grade, and you know it. You can see inside my mind. I'm a passable detective at best. Most of what I do is luck and inside information from ghosts. Finding Aemon is outside my wheelhouse."

Not to mention I had a big enough target on my ass as it was. Adding "demon finding" to my resume was one thing too many.

He pursed his lips as he assessed me, his mismatched eyes narrowing ever so slightly as he ran a scarred hand through his salt-and-pepper hair. "Your mind is made up then? You're sure?"

I wasn't sure about anything anymore—not about Aemon, the state of my mind, my safety, my job. Bishop's deal with Aemon—the one that healed my wounds and made it so the prince would never again enter my mind—seemed even more suspect the longer I thought about it. No demon would make that deal and most definitely not keep it after he'd been stiffed on his end.

I rubbed at the spot on my sternum that Aemon had touched. Even now it felt like I'd been branded, the skin still tender, although it appeared perfectly healthy.

And why would Bishop do that—put my life more at risk than it already was? Why would he make that deal with Aemon in the first place?

Everything about my life was on shaky ground. Everything.

"Positive."

He did that little tutting thing again, likely reading the thoughts that swarmed my mind rather than the actual words from my lips. "They said you were brave. That you'd rise to the challenge."

"They" could be anyone. "They" said a lot of things.

"Sorry to disappoint. Maybe if you'd asked me bearing gifts or food or coffee, the outcome would be different. Maybe if you'd asked *at all* instead of demanding. Or maybe my quota for answering bullshit demands of my time has been filled already today. Try again tomorrow."

But tomorrow would be booked, too—what with the council requesting my presence, a gaggle of witches ready for payback, a werewolf pack trying to start a war, and an ABI director trying to take me out. Oh, and don't forget that little thing called sleep.

*Man, I miss sleep.*

Maybe I'd actually get quality rest now that I wasn't being inhabited by a prince of Hell.

Deimos' eyes tightened at the corners as he clenched his jaw, the intimidation tactics back in full force. I fought to keep myself from rolling my eyes. Did he even give a shit that his son broke every rule demons had? Okay, so I didn't know *all* the rules, but asking consent was kind of a big one. Did he care that I'd just lost so much of myself?

Safety? *Gone.*

Security? *Had I ever had that?*

Sanity? *Waving bye-bye as we spoke.*

And here he was in my space asking for more? After everything that had been stolen from me? I had half a mind to follow through with that punching threat.

"Darby?" Bishop called in the middle of our little staring contest. "Who are you talking to?"

I swiveled on a foot, really wishing Bishop had stayed in the house. Sure, things were a little shaky, but I didn't want him hurt. And while demons couldn't enter homes uninvited, Deimos wasn't exactly a demon, and I didn't own the house. Maybe he was no safer inside than he was out here.

"Aemon's father," I answered. "Maybe go inside, yeah?"

Bishop's eyebrows rose on his forehead. "You're talking to a demon? You're sure?"

Slowly, I turned back to the deity in question, a wide smile on his scarred face.

"Not exactly," I replied, folding my arms over my chest.

Azrael had done this a time or two—made himself invisible to everyone else but me. My eyes narrowed all on their own. "You just had to make me look like a complete fucking nutter, didn't you?"

"Driving people insane is sort of my profession, you know. After all this time, I should be rather good at it."

"Lucky for me, people are already used to me talking to things they can't see. I'll give an A for effort, though." I gave the jerk a sweet Southern smile and a feigned accent to match. "Good luck finding your son."

The smile dripped from Deimos' face. "You'll be helping me—one way or another. It's best you figure that out." His gaze drifted from me to Bishop. "Sooner rather than later."

Then the bastard had the audacity to just up and disappear before I could ask what in the blue fuck he meant by that.

Gnashing my teeth, I whirled back toward the house, stomping my way up the porch steps in much the manner in which I'd gone down them.

"What was all that about?" Bishop asked, crossing his arms over his tight black T-shirt, his normally dark eyes flashing gold.

*To tell him or not to tell him.*

Sighing, I dropped my forehead against the valley between his pecs, relishing it more than probably necessary as he uncrossed his arms and wrapped them around me. I could stay here, say nothing, and maybe go get a nap. I really, really could. Forget how betrayed I'd felt at his deal with Aemon. Forget all the dominos poised to fall.

Unfortunately, honesty was sort of a failing of mine. And the fact that Deimos had intimated that maybe I wasn't the only one that was vulnerable made not saying anything a dick move.

Taking a deep breath, I let the truth go in one big gust. "I'm pretty sure I just got threatened by a god."

## 2

"**A**re you freaking kidding me?" I grumbled, staring at the big box in Sarina's arms. It was about the right size for a giant puffy dress, as if she'd known this whole time I'd be summoned to the council. "If there is a ball gown in there, I'm shooting you."

I couldn't think about Deimos and his not-so-subtle threat right then, or that I never did get that nap. The council had summoned me to a nonnegotiable black-tie only meeting. And what kind of a meeting was black-tie only, anyway?

Bullshit ones, that's what.

The thought of going into a blind meeting with entities I didn't know—in a ball gown no less—sounded like the absolute worst idea I'd ever heard of. Add that to Bishop's insistence on coming with me, even though his name had been nowhere on the invitation, and well…

Anxious didn't quite cover it.

"No, you won't. You'll understand exactly why I'm having you wear this, while keeping your gun right where I can see it," Sarina replied, an evil curl to her lips, practically daring me to reach for my weapon.

"I'm listening," I muttered, crossing my arms. She could speak her peace, but I wasn't wearing a damn dress. I'd filled my quota of skirt-wearing for the year at my father's funeral.

I was done.

Sarina crossed the bedroom and plopped the box on the bed, whipping off the lid with a flourish. Inside was a mound of blood-red fabric with glittering jewels peppering the bodice.

"Think about it. They're already going to paint you as an outcast," she cajoled, running a finger over the rather gorgeous applique. "You're a freaking demigod for one, and two, you're the first Warden in a handful of centuries. If you go in jeans or leather pants, the council will take it as a sign of disrespect. Plus, think about all the weapons you can hide under a skirt like that?"

With a skirt that floofy, I could fit a damn arsenal under there. I waved for her to continue. "Carry on."

"Now, they'll probably take all those weapons away from you, but if you don't pack them, council security will just strip-search you, and *no one* likes that."

I fought the urge to stomp my foot. Okay, I actually did stomp my foot, but could anyone really blame me? "You just said I could take an arsenal. What good is an arsenal if I can't actually use it?"

"Patience, Grasshopper. I've already thought of that," she said as she gently gripped the bodice and whipped it from the box.

Begrudgingly, I had to admit the thing was beautiful. Giant swaths of burgundy beaded applique covered the scarlet skirt, trailing all the way up the bodice. That said, the skirt was giant—far bigger than I'd originally thought while it had still been in the box. It was like the walls of the container were spelled to hold that much fabric.

Still stunned a dress could possibly be that big, I barely heard the knock on the bedroom door.

"Come in," Sarina called. "She's decent."

J and Jimmy waltzed through the entrance. "Decent?" J scoffed, running a hand through his perfectly coiffed dark hair, his pale-blue eye sparkling with mirth. "Not a day in her life."

Shooting a mock-irritated glare at my best friend, I stuck out my tongue for good measure. Yes, I was an adult—a super-classy, totally with-it, full-of-class adult. *Totally.*

Jeremiah Cooper and I had been best friends since we were in diapers, so if anyone knew my level of decency or maturity, it would be him.

"If anyone ruined me, it was you, jerk," I groused, bumping him with my hip hard enough to make him stumble.

J flipped me off but did so with a smile. "If you keep being an asshole, Jimmy will just take his gift back, won't you, babe?"

Jimmy Hanson was a giant of a man—though calling him a man was a slight stretch. The tall Fae kissed J's temple before folding himself into a bedside chair, giving him a patient smile all the while. "Probably not," he said, flipping his long hair behind a very pointed ear. "But that's only because she needs it."

He fished something out of his pocket, swinging the object by its chain from his long fingers. A burgundy jewel winked at me from an intricate setting as it swayed back and forth.

"Think of this like a bulletproof vest," he said, resting the silver-dollar-sized pendant on his palm. "If you can't have any weapons, at least you can have this. I've cloaked it enough—no one should even blink at it."

*Fluffy dresses and pretty jewels? Might as well call me* Cinderella.

Sarina rolled her eyes. "*Cinderella*, you are not. Well, maybe, if she said 'fuck' too much and carried a gun."

She wasn't wrong. "Quit reading my thoughts, weirdo. And I can complain inside my head all I want to, dammit."

But that necklace sure was pretty, and even though wearing it would almost certainly be torture, the dress was gorgeous. Begrudgingly—and gently—I took the dress from Sarina and slogged to the bathroom like I was off to the gallows. As soon as my guard was down, I was certain Sarina would be talking about makeup and hairdos.

While attempting to wriggle into a dress that size, I learned a few things about myself. One: beading was heavy, uncomfortable, and a certified pain in the ass. Two: there was no way on this earth or any other that I could possibly get it on by myself. For a gown as heavy as it was, it required an internal corset sewn into the bodice to keep everything up. Since the dress eschewed straps and my bust was minimal, without the corset, it wouldn't stay on without a dump truck of magic and even then...

After ten minutes of struggling, I pleaded for Sarina to come save me from the burgundy fabric. By the time she got the hook and eye closures all done up, I realized I needed to pee, and it was a race to see if I could hold it long enough to get out of the damn thing. On the second round, it took far less drama getting me into the dress, and even from the scant reflection in the bathroom mirror, I could tell it would be worth it—not that I'd admit it out loud.

We emerged from the confines of the bathroom—the door an actual struggle with the volume of the skirt—and I made a beeline for the full-length mirror, ignoring J's hooting and wolf whistles.

The woman in the mirror was a stranger. I still hadn't gotten used to the white hair or the odd glint to my blue eyes or the subtle glow to my skin, and that lent nothing to the fact I was in a red ball gown about to go talk to important people. Lifting my chin, I stared at my reflection, forcing myself to reconcile the woman in the mirror with the flat-chested, knobby-kneed teenager I'd been so long ago who saw ghosts and only had two friends. The dress's internal corset did fabulous things to my waist, making it seem far smaller than it actually was, while my bust appeared to have also gotten a boost.

The real question was whether or not I'd be able to wear this death-trap of a dress all night.

*I hope the council has wide-open entryways.*

"We can leave your hair down, I think. Maybe put

some glam waves in it?" Sarina mused, tapping her bottom lip. "Obviously, I'm not putting you in heels, but can I talk you out of combat boots?"

That hadn't even crossed my mind until then. "Absolutely not."

That's where I drew the line. My boots were staying. Period.

She gave me a sly smile in the mirror. "I figured as much."

Jimmy peeled himself from the chair to fit the necklace around my throat. The thick chain was short, the heavy stone hitting just an inch below my collarbone. He fastened the clasp, and with a golden wave of his fingers, magic settled over the metal.

"There," he said, dusting imaginary schmutz off his hands. "No one should say a word about it or even look at it twice. It should repel most spells, attacks, and whatnot."

I leveled him with a single raised eyebrow through the mirror. "You're working on one of those for your boyfriend, right?"

There had been too many times where I'd worried about the people in my life. It didn't seem fair that I got a magical bulletproof vest when J was swinging in the wind. The only non-magical person in the group was intensely bad about keeping his ass out of the fire.

Jimmy had the gall to wink at me but said nothing. That wink had better have been an affirmative, or there would be some serious hell to pay.

After Sarina's ministrations—or torture as I'd have liked to refer to it—I was now put together enough that she'd quit fiddling with me.

Glam waves? *Check.*

Red lip? *Check.*

Winged eyeliner sharp enough to cut someone and should be classified as a deadly weapon? *Also check.*

And if I happened to have strapped an arsenal to my thighs on the off chance a war broke out? Well, then, so be it.

It wasn't that I didn't believe Sarina when she said they'd take my weapons from me—I did. It was more that I hoped they wouldn't. Jimmy's necklace—while beautiful—didn't exactly instill the warm and fuzzies of safety when I'd be walking into a proverbial lion's den. The only bright spot was the look on Bishop's face when I came down the stairs *She's All That* style—only since I was wearing combat boots instead of heels, I did not trip at the base of the stairs and get caught by the handsome Freddie Prinze Jr.

His dark eyebrows damn near reached his hairline as his jaw went slack.

"Wow, Adler. Just... Wow." His voice was a low growl that promised very naughty times later.

Fighting the urge to blush at his solid appreciation of my outfit, I instead focused on how his shoulders filled out his crisp tux. As a woman who'd had to go stag to prom, this was a girlhood fantasy come to life. There was not a single teenage boy in Haunted Peak that could have pulled off a tux as well as Bishop La Roux.

Two hours before midnight—and right about the time I was attempting to figure out how to shove this damn dress into my Jeep to traverse the ass-end of Tennessee to get to the council—a black extended Escalade stopped in front of the Warden house. I shot a questioning look at Sarina.

"What?" She shrugged. "I am not letting you try to stuff a ball gown into your Jeep, and I worked too damn hard on that eyeliner to let you puke after shade jumping. A car service was the only way to go. Think of it like a break?"

The way she phrased it like a question made my lips quirk up just a bit. I couldn't say exactly how long it had been since I'd slept, but it had been a minute. Hell, just the thought of sleeping at all made me shudder. The last time I'd managed to get some rest, I'd ended up waking up on a grave. A break might not be in the cards for me.

I did manage a few moments of shut-eye in the back

of the limo, holding onto Bishop's hand as I rested against his shoulder. It really was a wonder how I could fall asleep anywhere with that much firepower strapped to my thighs, but I made it work. I had a feeling it could have been sweeter if I wasn't so up in the air about the last twenty-four hours.

By the time we arrived, I'd perked up a bit—the marginal security of the limo a sight better than the Warden house or my now-demolished home in Haunted Peak. At least with Bishop awake by my side and a faceless driver, I had the illusion of safety. And even though I couldn't quite drop off into dreamland, I was a sight more rested than I had been.

Right up until the SUV stopped and Bishop escorted me out.

Then *any* sort of rest went right out of the window.

## 3

"**A**re you carrying any weapons, ma'am?" the rather burly security guard asked, crossing his beefy arms over his chest as if he was prepared for me to lie.

Don't get me wrong, I was totally prepared to lie my ass off, but his face said I would be about the thousandth person to fib to him tonight, and he was having none of it. Cool gray eyes practically dared me to cross him, and coupled with his shiny bald head, he had a Caucasian Dwayne Johnson flair to him that made me really consider my options.

Moxie.

I would have to go with moxie.

Personally, I was ecstatic to delay getting inside the building. After pulling up in the limo and prying my dress from the vehicle, I'd been hit with a one-two punch of luxury that made me more than a little uncomfortable. Women and men—in finery I had never even thought of before—strode from their luxury cars and limousines like they were on their way to the red carpet. And it didn't matter that Bishop was whispering in my ear that everything would be all right—the stares from the other patrons were proving him wrong by the millisecond.

And no part of this even touched on the building itself.

I'd never seen a manor house outside of period dramas, but the ivy-coated, turret-having building—which seemed big enough to encompass a full city block—had to be one. The only other name was "castle," and as big as it was, there appeared to be a lack of a moat and drawbridge.

Lifting a perfectly shaped eyebrow at the guard—courtesy of Sarina—I gave The Rock Part Deux a conspiratorial smile and twirled a finger. "Would you walk into a place like this unarmed, sir?"

The Rock Two blinked at me before surveying the crowd and letting out a little huff. "No, ma'am, I can't say I would. Though, I'm still going to have to ask that you disarm yourself and submit to a pat down."

Sarina warned me this might happen, so I wasn't

exactly surprised, but I wasn't happy about it, either. However, given the giant TSA-style metal detectors, there was no way I would be getting through them without alarms going off.

Still... "Any chance of a freebie pass for being the Warden—"

"I was specifically told that everyone was to be searched regardless of status and no weapons of any kind could enter."

"And saying the beeping was due to a zipper—"

"Would be the tenth such excuse I've heard tonight." The guard sighed like this was the worst job in the world, and he'd really enjoy being anywhere else.

"Fair enough," I muttered. I'd done enough security as a beat cop to know this job sucked ass. And that had been with humans. Who knew what kind of power the arcane guests had? I sure as shit didn't want to find out the hard way. "I'll be getting these back, right?"

Rock shrugged. "Depends. If you're packing a WMD under that gown, probably not. But guns, knives, athames, and potions? Most likely."

The thought of rocking a weapon of mass destruction under my skirt never occurred to me but considering I could fit a damn tank under there, it wasn't exactly out of the question. As discreetly as I could, I lifted my skirt and pulled the throwing knives from my left boot, placing them in the TSA-looking bin that conveniently had my name printed on the plastic. Quickly following them was the .22 strapped to my right ankle, the 9mm at my right thigh, and the dagger at my left.

"Are you out of your mind?" Bishop hissed under his breath, staring at me like I'd grown another head—or like I was embarrassing him somehow. "Bringing weapons? *Here*? Are you *trying* to die?"

I had half a mind to flip him off—either that or shove one of my daggers under his thumbnail. "That's precisely what I'm trying *not* to do," I replied, fitting my fists to my hips—not that finding them with a skirt this big was easy. "The invitation said nothing about not bringing any weapons. After the week I've had, being armed is just smart."

*Like he doesn't have a backup weapon strapped to him somewhere.*

"Is that all, ma'am?" Rock asked with a small quirk to his lips.

I held up a finger before fishing the three small knives out of the bodice that I'd managed to fit against my skin without gouging myself. The tricky one was the blade in between my boobs, and I turned just slightly so as to not flash anyone as I gently pulled it free.

Doing a mental count, I nodded as I smoothed down

the skirt of my dress and adjusted the bodice. "There. That should be everything."

"You sure?" Bishop groused, rolling his eyes.

Opening my mouth to say something, someone else beat me to it.

"What crawled up his arse and died?" Hildy griped, his familiar Irish lilt nearly making me jump. He'd been MIA for most of the day, not wanting to hang around while I got all dolled up. What he'd been doing was anyone's guess, but a familiar face was a familiar face. Plus, him speaking my thoughts aloud was just a bonus.

Practiced as ever, I snapped my mouth shut, ignoring my ghostly grandfather *and* Bishop as I focused on the wand in the guard's hand. One would think he'd be holding a metal detecting wand, but no. No, the big, burly guard had a filigreed gold stick in his hand with an actual crystal embedded in the base. He swirled it around me as if he were tying a bow before inclining his head in an approving nod.

"You're good to go, ma'am." Rock flicked his gaze to Bishop, his expression turning to stone. "Sir, will you remove any weapons you may have on your person?"

Bishop straightened the bow tie on his tux, sniffing. "I didn't bring any."

Rock and I stared at Bishop like he'd done to me just a second ago. We were headed into an unknown situation, and he didn't bring so much as a letter opener? I would have called bullshit, but Rock was quicker on the draw.

"Sir, I was born at night, but it wasn't last night. All weapons must be surrendered prior to entry. Trust me, once I wave this wand, they'll burn hot enough to set fire to your clothes. If you keep being a dick about it, I won't put you out."

Hildy and I snickered. "Oh, I like this guard, lass. Much better than the—what do the kids call them these days?—*douche canoe*—you chose to date." Hildy shot Bishop a snide little lip curl like he was smelling rancid meat and rolled his eyes. "Are we sure about him, lass?"

I gave Hildy my best glare but said nothing. This wasn't the first time Hildy had made his feelings known about Bishop, but after the bargain with Aemon? Well, he'd been a lot more vocal about his misgivings.

And that was the problem, wasn't it?

It didn't matter that I hadn't wanted Bishop to set Aemon free. It didn't matter that I'd mentally begged him not to give Aemon what he wanted. It was more that one: he'd made the deal at all, and two? That he'd gone back on said deal and gambled with a Prince of Hell with my life on the line.

At least when Hildy had done it, he'd been betting on my sister to save me while keeping a demon in his cage.

Now that demon—or demigod as the case turned out to be—was on the loose. I rubbed at the spot on my chest where Aemon had touched me, the burn setting my teeth on edge as I tried not to slap Bishop upside the head.

"Fine," Bishop muttered, pulling the backup ankle piece from its holster, and smacked it into his own bin hard enough to make me wince.

*Who's the embarrassing one now?*

"Is that all, sir?" Rock asked, his derisive tone making my lips quirk.

Bishop appeared to consider the guard and his raised wand for a moment. Twisting his mouth in a petulant little sneer, he yanked a dagger from a hidden sheath in his jacket and slapped it next to the gun.

*That little hypocrite*, I thought while trying to keep the scorn off my face. I was starting to think coming by myself to this bullshit shindig would have been a better option—even if it would leave me without backup. It made me long for the days of J watching my six. At least when he gave me the stink-face, I could flick him on the forehead.

Rock did his wand wave, clearing my date, but before we could make it past him, he dropped a meaty paw on Bishop's shoulder and squeezed. "I want you to remember that there isn't a Bishop La Roux on the guest list," he threatened, the menacing whisper of his voice chilling me to the bone, and it wasn't even aimed at me. "You're here as her plus-one, and any time she decides she's had enough of your bullshit, she can easily tell one of the guards, and you'll get tossed out on your ass." Rock then straighten Bishop's jacket before brushing an invisible speck of lint off his shoulder. "You have a good night, sir."

Bishop's eyes went gold for a moment before he got ahold of himself and shoved past the giant of a man. I paused, letting my petulant date move ahead as I remained behind.

"What's your name?" I asked.

Rock narrowed his eyes at me but answered, "Björn, ma'am."

"Thanks, Björn. I appreciate the info and the assist." Hesitating, I asked, "It's safe here, right? No offense to you and your security skills, but I've had a rough few days."

"Then you know the importance of watching your back." Steely blue eyes assessed me for a moment. "And keeping people you can trust close."

My gaze strayed to Bishop's back as he plucked a champagne flute from a passing waiter's tray. Could I trust Bishop? Before Aemon, I would have said yes.

But now?

Add that to the fact if I was asking myself the question in the first place, the answer was pretty damn obvious.

*Shit.*

"Again, thanks, Björn. You have a good night. And," I paused, plucking a card from my satin clutch, "if you need anything, let me know." It was one of my old cards, but the name and number hadn't changed.

Frowning, he took it. "Will do, ma'am."

Nodding, I passed him, following Bishop into the venue as nerves clogged my throat. It wasn't just the fancy house and crazy number of people that had me contemplating stealing a food tray and running for the hills. More than anything, it was the sheer amount of trepidation I had for the unknown. Until a few days ago, I hadn't even known there *was* a council. Now here I was dressed in a frock, weaponless, and without backup, walking into a building that cost more than my lifetime salary.

With Hildy as my shadow, I strode through the entrance and toward a wide landing, praying for one of those waiters to show up. Booze, food, and for this whole night to be a memory would go a long way to easing my nerves.

*You've gone up against a whole coven of witches, an entire wolf pack, and a ghoul nest practically by yourself. How hard can walking into one little room be?*

My internal pep-talk was damn near drowned out by Hildy's cackling. "That big bastard really gave your boy toy a run for his money, didn't he? Would've loved seeing someone put the mage on his ass, though." Hildy's gray face pulled into an exaggerated pout before dawning into a grin again. "But the night's still young. If he's acting like a fecking eejit now, who knows what will happen?"

Fighting off rolling my eyes, I plucked a yummy morsel off a passing tray. As I reached a wide staircase, I nearly choked on the duck confit crostini I'd stuffed into my mouth whole. Before I could take the first stair, every single eye in the place trained themselves on me. Hell, even the string quartet in the corner stopped playing, the violinist flubbing her bow and creating a god-awful racket.

Hildy snickered for a second. "Tough crowd, lass. Was it somethin' I said?"

## 4

The delectable snack turned to ash in my mouth as I struggled not to run screaming from the weight of the stares. Seriously? Was this a bad '80s teen movie? Managing to gulp down the now-dry bite, I navigated down the stairs, doing my best not to break my neck with this stupid dress.

My god, was I a moron or what? What did I think would happen? That these people would welcome me with open arms, sleepovers, and pedicures or something?

Buzzing whispers replaced the silence, and thankfully, the band began playing again, but those stares? Oh, they were there to stay.

And where was my boyfriend, my date, the man who professed his love for me like a week ago, you ask? Well, he was at the bottom of the marble staircase, sipping his champagne, and staring at me just like the other chuckleheads in the room.

I had half a mind to slap the flute out of his hand and make a real scene. I was causing a spectacle already—a *teensy* little show couldn't hurt, right?

"Oh, there's the Baron of Cornwall. Or that's what he likes to call himself, the silly bastard," Hildy whispered, leeching some of my mounting embarrassment and hurt. He pointed out a rather downtrodden fellow with an off-center bowtie, holding a waiter's tray hostage as he shoveled the canapes into his mouth. "Warlock with too little power and more money than the Almighty is more like it. You know in 1504, he commissioned a witch to make a deal with a demon for more power. Poor sod ended up with a smaller pecker and half his properties gone."

It took everything in me not to giggle—a feat only possible because I was currently giving Bishop a death glare of epic proportions. His cool black gaze revealed exactly zero guilt for his prolonged tantrum. When he continued to sip his glass of fancy booze, I flicked the base, splashing his skin with the fizzy drink. It wasn't throwing a full glass in his face, but it would do in a pinch.

Innocently, I smiled at him, plucking my own flute

from a passing waiter. If he was going to act like an idiot, I'd fucking well treat him like one. I swear, if he was *Scooby-Doo*-style pulling the mask back, I'd prefer if he got the lead out.

Now-gold eyes flashed back at me, Bishop's hold on his magic failing as he pulled a handkerchief from his breast pocket. Wiping at his stubbled chin, he muttered, "Was that necessary, Adler?"

*Was that growl necessary?*

"Of course it was," I murmured into my glass, taking a sip of the crisp wine. The delicious, semi-sweet flavor was probably the most expensive thing I'd ever tasted. "And if *I* were acting like a bitchy toddler, I'd hope you'd call me on it as well."

I pivoted on my boot, allowing Hildy to keep rambling in my ear about people I didn't give two shits about, thanking my lucky stars I'd been smart enough to avoid heels.

"Over there is Hilda Von Strauss. Oldest blood mage on the continent. Went up against her in Chur before the Swiss went 'magic-free' and quit letting arcaners in. Humans think the whole country's neutral, but really they're a bunch of no-magic having wankers." Hildy flitted to my side, pointing a ghostly finger at an Amazon of a woman in a gown tight enough to classify itself as a sausage casing. "She was a force to be reckoned with, but I still beat her in the end. Bedded her, too, if memory serves."

With that one, my crostini almost came up, and I fought off the urge to gag.

Did I want dirt and distraction?

*Absolutely.*

Did I want tales of my grandfather's diddle conquests?

*No, the fuck I did not.*

A hand at my elbow interrupted my plans of mentally punting my grandfather out of the room. I stared down at the fingers gently circling my upper arm before allowing myself to meet Bishop's gaze.

His features painted in chagrin, he dropped a kiss to my exposed shoulder. A week ago, that would have been all he'd needed to do. Now? It felt false. I fought off the urge to shake his hold off my arm and punch him in the junk.

"I'm sorry, Adler," he whispered against my skin. "I was acting like an asshole."

Silently, I nodded before sipping my beverage. It was bad enough he'd tried to throw his weight around with security—which was a teensy step down from being rude to a waitress in my book—but then he'd left me to walk in here with all those stares by myself?

On top of what transpired yesterday?

There wasn't a sweet kiss and apology in the world that would win me over.

*Man, I wish J was here. At least he'd have been smart enough to bring a flask.*

"Take a gander at that pompous bastard," Hildy said, drawing my eye to a tall man with a posture so straight I feared he might actually have a stick up his ass. "High Alpha of the North American shifters. With a name like Leighton Whittaker IV, it's no wonder he looks like that much of a wanker."

*This coming from a man named Hildenbrand.*

"Did you know he lost Alpha for about three years in the 1730s after he got caught gambling away the family fortune?" he whispered like I wasn't the only person in the room that could hear him. "Huge mess, and his mother had to step in and run the lot of the shifters because his father was too in his cups to do it. Whole family are either gamblers, addicts, sex fiends, or letches. My kind of people, even if their leader is a huge stick in the mud now."

All of this was super fascinating—*not*—but I'd rather deal with Hildy's ramblings than Bishop. And I thought that right up until I spied a familiar face in the crowd.

I might have beef with Bishop—previous epithets professing our love or not—but August Theodore Davenport III? Well, I'd toss his cravat-wearing ass off a cliff with exactly zero remorse. Hell, I might even giggle if the occasion called for it.

Maybe even throw a party, too.

The slight blond man knifed through the milling patrons, making a beeline for me. Smartly, I tossed back the rest of my glass of wine and exchanged it for a full one as a tray passed.

Seriously? Where was a bottle of vodka when you needed it?

The director of the ABI strode with purpose, his posture as rigid as the frown on his face. Stopping just outside of touching distance, the short man pinned on a disdainful expression as he attempted to cow me just by his mere presence.

*Tough luck, buddy. Even the God of Torment couldn't intimidate me today.*

Studiously, I ignored him—as did Hildy—and continued listening to my grandfather spill all the arcane tea. Unfortunately, Bishop didn't get the memo, placing himself between me and his former boss.

"You have a lot of nerve to walk over here like you have the right," Bishop hissed, his whisper barely audible over the din of conversation and the band. He crowded the smaller man as if they were close to coming to blows.

I couldn't exactly blame Bishop. Davenport had

enlisted two witches to murder me and make it look like an accident. Anyone who cared for me at all would be doing the same. And while I should probably be up in arms and ready to throw down? Doing it in the middle of this shindig seemed poor form.

No, I'd get Davenport when he least expected it. When I exacted my revenge, it wouldn't be a fistfight in the middle of a crowd. It would be quiet, devastating, and everlasting. He'd curse me for the rest of this life and on into the next one.

But for now, I stared through the men like they weren't standing right in front of me—well, until the director started speaking.

"Do you honestly think she got summoned here because the council just wanted to throw a party?" Davenport jeered in Bishop's face, curling his lip in an almost snarl. "No. She has shit to answer for." He spared me a snide glare. "I had them summon you, get you all dressed up, and when they're done with you—"

"Are you quite finished?" I interrupted, finally meeting the director's gaze as I side-stepped Bishop. "I know exactly what you did, and when I'm done here, the council will know it, too. And after that?" I let loose a feral smile. "Well, I'll be sure to introduce you to someone who is *dying* to know how Aemon got free."

Davenport scoffed, his impolite snort rattling from

his aristocratic nose like a fucking trumpet. "No one is more powerful than the council," he chided, straightening his cravat. "No one."

That just showed how much he knew.

The director—in all his worldly wisdom—didn't know that Aemon was a Prince of Hell. That kind of a title came with a full-god daddy who was more versed in torture than I even wanted to contemplate.

"Again, sweetheart," I cooed, my tone as sweet as molasses, "you fail to account for deities in your calculations. Aemon's daddy is looking for him. Do you know who that is? 'Cause I do, and he's damn near desperate to find out who fucked up enough to let his son out of his cage. Now, I don't want to point fingers, but..." I trailed off, shrugging.

That was a lie. I really, really wanted to point a finger at the giant flaming turd that was Davenport, but I'd much rather tattle on him to the council first. Then after they were done with him, I'd call out for Deimos and show him who was responsible for his son slipping his leash.

It was bad enough the director had sent two witches that couldn't fight their way out of a paper bag, but a kill order? Had that really been necessary? And who did that? I mean, who knew what would have happened if those witches had actually *managed* to kill me? I'd been hopped up on power all on my lonesome—what kind of destruction would that demon turning incorporeal have wrought?

*What kind of destruction is he doing now?*

I shoved that thought down in favor of watching Davenport's face pale as his smug grin slipped just a bit. Precedent had shown him I wasn't one to bluff, and I couldn't wait to prove it to him again.

"You really think I'll wear this?" he asked, his ego bolstering his fragile hold on reality. "I'm not the one who got possessed or let a demon loose."

My grin widened. "No, that lands on Agent Bancroft who dealt with Aemon directly and set him free." I tapped my chin, pretending to forget the events that had transpired just a day ago. "Who sent her again?"

"You can't prove anything."

*The hallmark statement of guilty men everywhere.*

"Can't I?" I tilted my head to the side as I reached out a hand to straighten the small man's cravat. "I wouldn't bet on it."

Another hush washed over the crowd, pulling my gaze away from Davenport. At the far end of the room, the patrons parted and a stream of arcaners trailed in a single-file line. As soon as each one of them stepped into the space, a familiar buzzing of power raced over my skin and into my brain—speaking of long lives and deaths too far out to see.

If I had a doubt as to who these people were, that would have told me volumes.

*The council.*

And at the end of a decently long line of arcaners, strode a very tiny woman inside a child's body—blond ringlets and all.

Ingrid.

Fucking.

Dubois.

## 5

I couldn't say having an ally as awesome as Ingrid on the council was a bad thing—especially with Davenport's bitchy ass trying to tattle on me. Being as old as he was, the likelihood that he had more than a few somethings under his sleeve was a damn definite.

What was even more probable? Him finding new and more inventive ways to murder me.

But my pint-sized, older-than-dirt vampire ally had just had her favorite home burned to the ground on my watch. I didn't exactly see good things with that. More like she'd kick my ass for not ripping that wolf alpha's head off and punting it into outer space.

Given how fucked up that pack was, I couldn't say I blamed her.

The stream of thirteen members marched past us toward the marble staircase. A barrel-chested man dressed in robes, complete with a brocaded cape, positioned himself in the center of the group as the rest fanned out around him. In his left hand was a long gold staff, the top capped with a radiant crystal bigger than my fist, the blue light casting an eerie glow on the room. He raised the staff in the air before slamming it against the first marble stair.

Three knocks and the whole of the room melted away. Gone were the rich tapestries and chandeliers, missing were the waiters and orchestra. Hell, even the champagne flute in my hand disappeared. And that said nothing of the drop in my belly that told me we weren't in Kansas anymore.

Now the lot of us—the council, Davenport, patrons, and all—were in a giant ballroom. The ceilings had to be thirty feet tall with golden runes embedded in the plaster. Each one glowed with heat as they burned bright with magic.

A sea of windows sat behind a raised platform, the thirteen members of the arcane council sitting in backless velvet chairs that seemed more than a little uncomfortable. Ingrid's chair matched the rest, her child-sized legs swinging as they failed to reach the floor.

The crowd began to buzz with excitement, fevered whispers humming like a hive of bees filled the room until the man banged his staff once more.

"I call this meeting to order," he boomed, his voice so loud, he might as well have screamed it in my ear.

I—along with the rest of the room—winced, zipping my trap shut. Hildy, though, had no such compunction.

"Was that bleeding necessary? Damn near rose me from my grave with that shite." My grandfather stuck his ghostly pinkie in his ear and wiggled it as he continued griping. "But Horus was always a pretentious bastard. A fecking staff, you prick? Like that will give you any more power."

Horus narrowed his eyes in my direction, his irises glowing an eerie yellow. I didn't know what species of arcaner the staff-wielding jerk was, but I had a feeling I was about to find out.

"Warden Adler," he called, the decibel of his voice not lowering a bit. "Step forward."

*Oh, joy. Just what I always wanted. To be more of a spectacle than I already am.*

There wasn't a time in my life where I wanted to be called to the carpet—or marble, as it were—but after the last week? I'd rather dip my toes in boiling oil.

Dutifully, I skirted around Bishop and Davenport, striding to the open space in front of the dais like I was walking to the gallows. Once there, I figured I was supposed to bow or something, but since no one deigned to give me an etiquette lesson, I didn't so much as incline my head.

A pit of dread yawned wide in my belly as the silence dragged on. Day one in my tenure as Warden and I'd pissed off a pack of wolves, set a demon free, and ten people got burned to death.

Okay, so technically speaking, I wasn't the one who set Aemon free, but I had a feeling no one else was going to see it that way.

I was *killing* this Warden thing, I tell ya.

Killing. It.

Posture straight and chin high, I studied each of the arcaners on the stage. Ingrid was at the outside edge of the group, her small childlike body encased in a poofy dress and Mary Janes, her pale-blonde hair in ringlets. Next to her were a trio of women. Each one was severe, dressed to the nines, and looking at me like I'd just fucked their husbands, shit on their front lawns, and pissed in their coffee all in the same day.

After them were a pair of men. One sat sideways in his seat with a leg over the armrest, a loafer-clad foot swinging in the breeze. He was the only one who still had booze, too, taking turns between sipping the bubbly and plucking grapes off the bunch in his hand with his teeth. He wore a half-buttoned white shirt under an honest-to-god smoking jacket, his tie loose around his neck.

The other wasn't even looking at me. No, he was staring at the impertinent shoe that seemed to be getting closer and closer to him each time it swung. Cold green eyes narrowed with each pass until a small ball of blue magic formed at his fingertips. He raised a raven eyebrow in warning, which went blithely unheeded, until that ball zapped the man's foot.

This earned him a grape to the face, beaning him right in the cheek.

On the other side of Horus was a quartet of men— each one dressed in a different color. The one in the red tux sported black eyes, black hair, and skin an odd shade of orange. And were those horns? The one in green had blond hair, yellow eyes, and had what appeared to be moss growing on the side of his face. Next to him was a man in blue, his hair was just a few shades lighter than his suit, and he was chugging from a gallon jug of water like he was dying of thirst. The last man was in yellow, his red wind-blown hair tangled around his face as he studied me with intense scrutiny.

The last two arcaners appeared bored to tears. The dark-haired male sat leaning to one side, his stubbled chin on his fist as if he'd rather be anywhere else. His pale eyes were half-lidded as if he were a few moments away from slipping into a nap. The woman, though, was a whole other matter. She held a power signature of an ancient, as her red-cast eyes trained themselves on me.

Okay, so I'd pissed some people off. Goodie.

Flicking my gaze back to Horus, I waited for him to continue. He'd been the one to call me to the center of the room. Hopefully, he'd get on with this bullshit. Yep. Anytime now.

Finally coming to the realization that I wasn't going to bow, curtsey, or beg for mercy, Horus cleared his throat, banging that blasted staff on the marble again before taking his seat.

"Warden Adler, do you know why we have summoned you here today?"

I couldn't help it. I raised an eyebrow, waiting for him to get decently uncomfortable before answering. "If Auggy here is to be believed," I replied, hooking a thumb at Davenport, "it's because he *made* you summon me, but I highly doubt someone with your abilities can be made to do anything."

Horus' tan face reddened, and his gaze shot past me to Davenport.

*Bet that boasting you just did is about to bite you in the ass, isn't it, Auggy?*

"Is that not the case, then?" I asked, giving the staff-wielding man a winsome smile.

Out the corner of my eye, I spied Ingrid's shoulders heaving with silent laughter, her hand clapped over her mouth so as to not let the giggles free.

"No," Horus growled. "This council has summoned you to discuss the tumultuous events from the last twenty-four hours."

*No shit, Sherlock.*

"Aww," I whined, painting a pout on my lips, "I thought you guys were welcoming me to the fold." I snapped my fingers in a false chagrin. "Darn."

The grape guy snickered outright, and Ingrid ducked her head, her shoulders shaking harder.

Horus raised an equally menacing eyebrow, mirroring me. "You seem to think sass and plucky humor will save you here. I assure you it will not."

"Save me?" I scoffed, setting my shoulders. "*Save* me? I've had this job for all of one day and I'm already being called in for whatever the fuck this is. But you let Douchey McFuck Clown run the ABI into the ground for how many years, and he gets nothing? I don't know who the fuck you think I am, but the one, I am not."

"Not the one, huh?" Horus barked, rising from his chair and taking a step down the dais so he could look down on me. "So you're not the one who enraged the alpha of the largest pack in the country? If not you, then who?"

Not to be cowed, I stepped closer, too, staring right into his glowing yellow eyes. "You mean the pack who killed three humans and seven witches in two days? That pack? The one who set fire to two buildings, drawing human attention? That one? *Yeah*, I angered that alpha." I fit my fists on my hips as I took another step closer. "But angering him was a far sight better than letting his weak ass continue getting railroaded by his own pack."

*Yeah, I said it.*

"I was given this job a day ago with no training, no explanation, and a wing and a fucking prayer to work shit out on my own. You got a problem with how I do business? Great. I'll go back to my home, job, and life, and you can figure out how to solve a string of murders in a single day damn near by yourself. Good luck."

Grape guy actually fell out of his chair laughing then, his guffaws echoing against the high domed ceilings which really pissed old Horus off. The barrel-chested man flew down the remaining steps, his staff and its eerie glow aimed right for me.

He never quite made it, though. Before he shuffled down the last step, he got hit by a tiny, blonde missile. Tackling him right to the marble, Ingrid had her fangs in his throat before the man could blink. Horus' color leeched from his skin, his tan face turning gray in seconds. When she'd drank her fill, Ingrid yanked her fangs back, fit her small hands against his cheeks, and snapped his neck with about as much fuss as clipping a hangnail.

The rest of the members didn't seem too surprised at Ingrid's antics, but the crowd sure as shit did—shouts and whispers alike buzzed through the room until Ingrid whipped her head up, her eyes red and veined and her mouth a bloody mess. She licked her fingers clean, and the room as a whole shut the fuck up.

*Smart.*

A moment later, Horus' ghost slowly lifted from his body, picking himself up off the marble as he stared at his withering corpse like he'd never contemplated that death had ever been an option. He reached for Ingrid, stumbling on his incorporeal feet when he slid right through her. Confused, he kept trying until I shoved him away from her with my mind.

"There," Ingrid said, sighing as she dusted off her hands. "Now that's done." Then she snatched the staff from the ground, tossing it at the severe woman with red eyes. "I hope you do better than he did. I'd hate to tell my queen her maker couldn't handle the job."

That caught my attention. Magdalena Dubois had

been made by Bishop's grandmother almost three thousand years ago. A famed blood mage, even I had heard of Lise Dubois. Lise caught the staff as if it weighed nothing, giving the overly ornate thing a look of derision. Ingrid seemed to have beef with her queen's maker, but I had a feeling it was more the absolute hate she had for the blood mage's grandson than anything else.

Then again, Ingrid was older than Jesus himself, so it was anyone's guess what squabbles were afoot.

Lise shifted her gaze from the staff to just past me, her derision not budging an inch. I wanted to follow the path of her eyes but knew exactly who she was looking at.

*Ouch. Poor Bishop.*

As much as I wanted to toss his dumbass off a cliff, my heart still hurt for him. Getting that kind of look from your grandmother? That was made of suck. I had to do *something*.

"Super. Now that that's done, why don't you get this bullshit show on the road so I can get out of this stupid dress."

Not my finest segue, but it worked well enough since Lise was now staring at me.

"Fair enough, Ms. Adler," Lise announced, her French accent thick as molasses. Rising from her chair, she glided over the marble to stand in front of Horus' former one. "I don't care about the wolf business. You were justified in your actions, and I agree—the alpha was weak. While I would have preferred a more permanent solution to that particular problem, your choice to spare the lives of the guilty makes no difference to me."

One of the women next to Ingrid's position growled, jumping from her seat. Lise shot a glare over her shoulder, silencing her instantly before shifting her gaze back to me.

"What I—and I think all of us here—want to know is how you managed to set a demon free."

*Well, shit.*

## 6

To throw Bishop under the bus, or to not throw him under the bus...

"Would you like the whole sordid tale or the Cliff's Notes version?" I asked, rubbing at my temple. What I really wanted to do was steal Grape Guy's seat and take a load off. But doing so with a room full of witnesses would probably be poor form.

And why did I have to come here with an audience, getting all dressed up to boot? Was it so I couldn't fight back? Was it so there would be plenty of witnesses to my demise?

This job was for the fucking birds.

"The highlights would be more expedient," Lise replied, a small smile pulling at the corner of her lips.

*At least she's having a good time.*

"Super," I muttered. "Well, about a week ago, in the midst of a coven of witches trying to rip a whole in the fabric of this realm, I managed to get myself possessed. Old Davenport here," I accused, hooking my thumb once again at the cravat-wearing asshole himself, "knew all about it, kept that info to himself, and instead of telling me, exorcising me, or being helpful at all, decided to order two ABI agents to take me out. Off the books, I presume."

Lise didn't give me much more than a pair of raised eyebrows, so I continued.

"When that went south for them, one of those agents made a deal with the demon, set him free from the box he'd been buried in, I got exorcised, and here the fuck we are." I glanced at my bare wrist, pretending to tell the time. "That was about twelve hours ago." Directing my gaze from Lise to Bishop, I asked, "Did I leave anything out?"

Yes, I totally left off the part where Bishop played chicken with a demon and lost with my life on the line, but who's counting? Gratefulness and guilt washed over his features before his mouth lifted into a half-grin.

"You forgot about the agents blowing up your house, solving ten murders, and winning a combat challenge with a werewolf," Bishop answered, ticking off the items on his fingers, "but you got the broad strokes."

I nodded before meeting Lise's eyes. "That's about it."

"It's utter horse shit is what it is," Davenport finally chimed in, idiotically stepping into the open space beside me. "She freed that demon herse—"

Davenport's bold-faced lie was cut off by my fist in his gut—a shot he never saw coming because he'd been too busy lying his ass off to the council. Did he honestly think I would just sit here and take the bullshit he'd been spewing?

*I think the fuck not.*

My hand found a hold in his perfectly coiffed hair, yanking his head up and back as I made the little shit look at me. "Tell the truth, you prick, or I'll pluck your eyeballs from your skull with my bare hands and feed them to the fucking crows."

Was that level of violence necessary? *Probably not.* But I was done with this shit. I was done with the fluffy dresses and no food and zero sleep, while the room at large judged me for something I couldn't control. I was done with no backup and not being able to trust anyone and losing the people I cared about.

I. Was. Done.

Thrusting Davenport forward, I made him face the council.

"Are you sure you want to be doin' this, lass?" Hildy asked, his note of caution ill-timed as ever.

I tossed him a glare before focusing on the assembled judges, council members, assholes, *whatever*. "Auggy here wants to tell the truth," I seethed through gritted teeth. "Don't. You?"

"Warden Adler, kindly unhand the director, please?" Lise asked, though the question was more like a demand.

"Sure thing. But first." I stalled, shaking Davenport's head like a maraca. "Was it my fault that Aemon was set free?"

"No," he gasped, his hands latching onto my wrists.

"Whose fault is it?" I persisted, tightening my hold, and threading a little power into my voice.

He hissed as some of the strands gave way, tearing from his scalp. "Bancroft. She made the deal."

I lifted my skirt with my free hand just enough so I could plant a boot in his back and kick his dumb ass away from me. Davenport landed on his hands and knees at the base of the dais, a chunk of his hair still in my fingers. Fluttering them, I watched with a sick sort of fascination as the strands floated to the floor.

"Well, I've heard enough," one of the uptight women from the council griped as she rose from her seat. "You claim that the witches were tr—"

Ingrid, Grape Guy, and his friend all stared at the woman like she'd lost her mind. But it was Ingrid herself that put the woman in her place. "Oh, shut the fuck up, Astrid. I was there. Those crazy bitches almost killed us all. And the ghouls were backing them up. All this has been hashed out already and you know it. Stop bringing up old shit." The small vampire faced off against the raven-haired beauty. "The only person on this council who doesn't believe it, is you. Darby was well within her rights to disband that coven, and the Monroe nest has been a boil on our asses for years. Let. It. Go."

*So much for needing immunity for my crimes…*

But Astrid had zero self-preservation instincts because she doubled down like a pro. "She kill—"

"For the love of all that is holy, Astrid. She was defending the realm from utter ruin. Sit. Down," Lise griped, smacking the staff against the marble.

As if there was a pull string tied to her ass, Astrid reclaimed her seat, but she didn't look happy about it.

Grape Guy shot me a winsome smile before tossing another piece of fruit in his mouth. "Can she come to all our meetings?" he asked Lise. "It's way more fun than normal."

"No offense," I said, pinching the bridge of my nose, "but if formal attire is a requirement, I'd rather skip them if I'm being honest."

Grape Guy shrugged before munching more fruit. "Party pooper."

"We aren't discussing the witch business," Lise grumbled. "We're talking about the demon. You say Agent Bancroft was sent to kill you, yes, but you still allowed yourself to be possessed in the first place. You still set a demon free. Whether the agent made the deal or not, as Warden, it is your responsibility to watch over the city of Knoxville and its surrounding area. A demon is running free on your watch, child. That does not speak highly of your ability to do this job."

What was I supposed to do? Turn back time? Flip this council off and go after him? What?

"Have you ever been possessed, Madam Dubois? Have you ever had something inside you, taking over your body and wreaking havoc?"

Lise contemplated this for a moment, likely flipping through her three millennia worth of memories. "No, I cannot say I have."

"And you've been around a while. You're powerful. You have esteem and friends, and enough allies to boot, right? So finding a demon for you would be easy, right? I mean, you don't have to heal, or grieve, or sleep, or get called into a bullshit council meeting that required black fucking tie. Finding a demon for you would be a snap.

Right? A blood mage such as yourself, you could do this with your hands tied behind your back and blindfolded."

She pursed her lips, assessing me as she took her seat once again. "I see your point."

"I don't," the bored-looking man on the end muttered. "She's a demigod for fuck's sake. She could have told us all to fuck off, but instead, she decided to get dressed up and come here. Make it make sense."

Parting my lips, it was on the tip of my tongue to agree with him, when darkness swept the room. Scared shouts and murmurs of fear rippled through the crowd. The glittering lights flickered out as a wave of power washed over me. In the next instant, a man stood in between me and the council, his crisp suit and salt-and-pepper hair giving him away before he ever turned around.

Then the lights flared back to life and the crowd really lost it. A few women screamed, and that was before they even got a good look at the man.

It really would figure that this night could get worse. I mean, why not? I'd already gotten my pee-pee slapped, why not bring in the big guns and mow me down?

Behind me, it sounded like there was a stampede going on. Frowning, I turned, watching as the patrons clambered from the room like their asses were on fire.

By the time I righted my gaze, Davenport had bounced out, too.

*Great.*

Deimos pivoted on a heel and stalked right over to me, a sly smile on his lips. Stopping just short of bowling me over, he leaned down to whisper in my ear: "Long time, no see, Darby. How's your night panning out?"

I had the strongest urge to flip him off, but refrained by the skin of my teeth. "Just peachy. And you? Find sonny-boy yet?"

Deimos' mismatched eyes lit with humor. "You know that's not my job," he corrected. "It's yours."

*The fuck it is. Find him yourself, you prick.*

He didn't react to my insult, and simply turned, addressing the council. "I'm disappointed," he began, clucking his tongue like a disheartened papa, staring at his naughty children. "When Darby said she needed to postpone her search for my son to honor the council, I had no idea she would be treated with such disdain."

My eyes narrowed all on their own at the sheer amount of bullshit coming from the man's mouth. I'd told him nothing of the council trip, and I know for damn sure honoring the council had never once crossed my thoughts.

"Given the disruption my son has caused, I had no

issue with her presence here—especially since she could need assistance in the task. But so far, she's been attacked, belittled, and challenged." He tutted again, shaking his head. "And here I thought you lot were smarter."

Astrid stood once more, facing off with the God of Torment like she was three crayons shy of a full box. "She's the idiot who set your son free. Why should we help her? She should clean up her own mess."

The witch even crossed her thin arms over her chest as if that cemented her statement.

Grape Guy looked at her, whipped his head to Deimos, and then smartly got the hell out of the way, still munching on his fruit and sipping his drink like he was about to watch a pay-per-view cage match.

Deimos regarded her with about as much joy as he would dog shit on his polished dress shoe. "And you are?"

Why he was asking, I didn't know. He could read her mind. He probably knew every facet of her personality, entire life history, and where she'd end up when she died.

When she opened her mouth to answer, he held up his hand. "It was a rhetorical question. I don't actually give a shit." He shifted his gaze to Lise. "Warden Adler has already agreed to help me find my son, and this farce of a meeting is getting in the way of that. Is there anything else you need from her, or do you plan on enforcing those sanctions you have rolling around in your brain?"

Lise's eyes rounded before narrowing to slits. "Save for the demon business, Warden Adler has done a commendable job in her short tenure. If she has agreed to search and apprehend your son, then we as a council have nothing to sanction. She is free to do her duties as she sees fit."

As one, the rest of the council stood—save for one tiny vampire—and filed off the stage as if the move was choreographed. But I couldn't focus on my friend. No, I was too busy staring at the smirking god who was walking toward me.

He leaned in, whispering once more in my ear, "I told you that you'd end up looking for my son." His smile stretched wide across his face. "And would you look at that? Now you are."

Of course I was.

*Why not?*

## 7

While I struggled not to flip off the God of Torment, Ingrid finally rose from her chair and moseyed on over. Thankful for the reprieve, I didn't even give her a look of censure when she stuck out her tongue at Bishop.

Since the two had never gotten along, I figured the ship for her to give a shit about my disapproval had sailed.

"I'm having someone collect your weapons," she began, easing a teensy part of me that still felt naked at the lack of protection. "They'll be along shortly."

Totally forgetting our audience, I gave the small vamp a hug, just managing to refrain from kissing her on the cheek. "You're a lifesaver. Literally."

In a roundabout way, I was referring to the ashes of

the man still piled in a heap near the dais. Thankfully Horus' ghost had skedaddled, leaving only Hildy's buzzing in my mind.

"Well, Horus had it coming. If there's anything I hate more than a power-hungry man, it's one who can't take criticism."

I simply blinked at her, knowing his attack on me was in no way the real reason he'd met his end. But we were in mixed company, and if she was going to tell me, it wouldn't be with a man she hated and an actual god in the room.

"Fair enough. Was the council really going to sanction me?" I asked, changing the subject.

Ingrid rolled her eyes. "Not if I can help it. Lise had to do something to act like she's in charge now. Sanctions are about as low on the reprimand ladder as it gets. And being possessed against your will isn't your fault." She shot an accusing glare at Deimos.

Before she could try to attack a god, I asked, "And Davenport? Please tell me someone somewhere is going to do something about that asshole." I crossed my fingers on both hands, holding them up so she could see. "And please don't make it be me. I have enough on my plate as it is."

Her eyes bled to scarlet as a scary smile pulled at her

lips. "Don't you worry about him. His days are numbered—trust me."

Deimos' lips quirked, and he gave the tiny vamp a respectful nod of his head. Whatever was running through Ingrid's mind was mighty impressive to the God of Torment—a fact that made my stomach turn. I guessed I could cross vengeance against Davenport off my to-do list. That shit appeared to be covered.

Ingrid's head whipped to my right, and she took off, bidding us a hasty, "Excuse me," as she left.

"I could have sworn you said you weren't going to go looking for Aemon," Bishop groused, breaking the silence. "I believe your exact words were: 'Not if Jesus himself comes down from on high and commands it.' Or did I miss something?"

I couldn't help it—I had to giggle at the sheer audacity and complete idiocy of the words that just fell out of his mouth. Sobering, I pointed to Deimos and asked, "You can see him, right?"

Bishop followed my finger to Deimos and nodded. "Sure can, but the last time you went up against his son, you damn near died. Two agents did die. Sarina and I almost got beaten to death, and I don't know what mojo he put on Hildy, but I can't assume it was good. You see where I'm going with this?"

I didn't want to bring up that he was the reason I'd almost died, but Hildy had no such compunction.

"Oh, don't act like you're a saint in all this, boy," my grandfather hissed, becoming solid as he was frequently wont to do. "You damn near got her killed when you welched on that deal. If his son didn't take pity on my girl, she'd be dead and buried right now. You played chicken with her life, ya fecking gobshite, and if she was smart, she'd toss ya out on yer arse and save herself the trouble of guttin' ya like a fish."

Hildy's skull cane glowed with power as his body seemed to swell in size. The lights flickered, as did his form, his eyes taking on a dark hue as the shadows roamed closer and closer to us.

"I'll be watching ya, mage. One toe out of line and I'll do the honors myself. I don't give a ripe shite that it'll send me to his domain," he growled, gesturing to the resident god in the room.

If I didn't know better, I would have sworn Hildy was turning, and it stung in a way that nearly took all the breath from my lungs. If Hildy turned into a poltergeist, that was it. There was no coming back from that—no way I could fix what was broken in him. I'd have to send him on, and...

I didn't know if that was something I'd ever be able to do. Not after Dad.

"Hildy," I croaked—something I hadn't done since I was a teen and he'd learned what my high school nemesis had done to me.

At the sound of my voice, the darkness lifted, and my grandfather peeled his gaze from Bishop's to look in my direction. "Lass?"

"Maybe you need a break. Go look in on J and Jimmy for me, okay? I've got this. Promise."

Swallowing hard, he nodded, returning to his normal grayed-out see-through self. "You're right, lass. I'll be going soon. You keep an eye on him, you hear? No one in their right mind would have done that, lass. I don't trust him. Not that I did before, but at least..." He shook his head, not deigning to continue. But I had an idea of what he would say.

At least a week ago, he trusted that Bishop actually gave a shit if I lived or died.

He trusted that Bishop wouldn't play with a demon when my life was on the line.

He trusted that Bishop loved me enough to keep me safe.

*Me too, buddy. Me. Too.*

The next instant, Hildy popped out of view, hopefully transporting himself to a place far from here with way less stress. Maybe he'd conjure himself up a tropical drink and stick his toes in the sand somewhere. If he was smart, he'd take a vacation.

Our family had never been the smart ones, though.

"Trouble in paradise?" Deimos quipped, and I couldn't stop the urge to flip him off this time.

"Oh, fuck you," I snapped, unable to look at either of the men. I could feel Deimos smiling, and that was bad enough, but Bishop?

If I reassured Bishop, he'd think what he'd done was okay, and I just couldn't do it again. The first time, I hadn't processed it yet, and now... now my rage ticked up a notch each time I thought about it.

But if I continued staring at anything but him, I'd hurt him, and the fact I was worried about harming the man who'd injured me—even though I loved him—made me want to scream.

In the tumult of my bullshit emotions, Ingrid saved my bacon, arriving just in time to pass my weapons off. I accepted my bin with a muttered "Thank you," while Bishop snatched his from her hands without so much as a "How do you do."

"You're welcome," she muttered while giving Bishop a healthy dose of side-eye. "You have my number if you need me. Try to stay breathing, will ya?"

Chuckling darkly, I muttered, "That's the plan. And take your own advice. Those wolves are freaking crazy. I hope you're taking extra precautions."

Ingrid rolled her eyes. "Oh, I am. Trust me."

With that, she swiveled on a heel and sped out of the room, leaving me in a space filled with a boatload of tension and a demon to find.

"All right, *Obi Wan*, where should we start the search for your long, lost son? A brothel, a pile of bodies, what?" Rather than sparing either man a glance, I started rearming myself, slipping knives back in sheaths and guns in holsters. I forwent sticking the three blades back in the bodice of my dress, preferring to room them with the throwing knives.

When Deimos failed to answer, I finally looked up, instantly annoyed at his smirking face. "Are we playing charades here? If so, can I at least get a hint?"

The god just crossed his arms over his chest, seeming to wait patiently. It was more like he was trying to wind me up, but I wasn't going to take the bait. "Fine. Wanna tell me how it got stuffed in the box in the first place? Nice piece of handiwork there."

Deimos' smile widened. *Okay, so I was getting warmer.*

"Maybe you should study that handiwork," he offered like he was speaking to a child.

I pinched my brow, desperately trying to stave off the headache that was worming its way into my skull. "This isn't a game, you asshole, nor is it 'fuck with Darby' time. You want your son found? You're going to have to work with me here. I know you love tormenting people, but if you could shelve that part of your personality for me, that'd be great."

The god stayed silent, his grin practically jubilant as he stared at me.

"Fine. Study the damn box. I got it."

"Finally," Bishop huffed. "Something I can actually help with."


Rather than take the hour-plus trek in the limo to Haunted Peak Memorial Cemetery, I allowed the God of Torment to spirit me there while Bishop followed on his own steam. As soon as my feet touched down, I was arrested by two facts. One: traveling with Deimos was a sight better than shade jumping with Bishop. Not only did I not want to hurl my guts up, but I also wasn't completely disoriented when we landed.

And two?

I in no way wanted to be anywhere near this cemetery ever again.

Less than a day ago, I'd almost died here. Two people did die here. Sure, it was all clean and tidy now, the blood and broken earth long gone—as was the box that had housed Aemon. Unerringly, my feet picked through the headstones toward the grave that used to be his—the near blackness of the night not hindering my sight one bit.

Bishop had done most of the legwork cleaning up the mess, decomposing the dead agents to ash before reburying the coffin. There was no evidence, no bodies, no nothing, and that fact brought me relief and made me sick all at the same time.

The cop in me hated it.

The part of me that could get tried for murder, though? She was happy as a clam.

Shivers raced over my skin as I stared at the headstone, and I rubbed at my exposed arms to beat back the chill. It was a balmy night as we edged on into late spring, but even through the metric ton of fabric, dread still reached me.

I couldn't even ask Bishop to raise the damn box, either—the sheer lunacy of it zipping my lips tight. The best I could do was shoot Bishop a pleading expression and hope he understood the assignment.

He tipped his chin in a truncated nod before black swirls of his power raced over his fingers and up his arms. A few moments later, the coal-black box with its scarlet sigils sprang from the earth as if the ground itself were shunning it. In the darkness, the red sigils glowed bright, making me gulp.

I rubbed at the spot where Aemon had touched me again—the pain more acute so close to his former home —and studied the markings. I didn't bother with the giant ones on the walls of the box—no, I focused on the lock that kept him sealed, the ring of blood-red carvings smoothed with age.

Sigils could sometimes be tough to decipher because there were some that followed a language like Nordic runes, and others that were just made up by the caster.

But a few of these markings?

They reminded me of a set of sigils carved into a very specific ring. One that had been resting snuggly at the base of my thumb until just a few days ago. The same ring that was now embedded in my sister's flesh.

"Azrael put your son down?" I whispered, gritting my teeth against the shiver of fear that rattled my bones. It was one thing to have this all be an accident. It was quite another for Aemon—and maybe his father—to want payback.

Humans, wolves, and witches I could fight. Hell, I'd throw down with ghouls and my own family if need be. But a god and his son?

*I might as well die now and save everyone the trouble.*

"He made the lock, yes," Deimos said, practically

gleeful at my raised blood pressure and fear-addled mind. "But to ease your fears, I asked him to."

"Care to share anything else? It's not like I can ask dear old dad about it since he's dead and all."

And didn't that just feel like I'd been gut-punched. Because thinking about Azrael made me think of Dad. And that just sucked.

"And yet," he murmured, his smile as wide as ever, "his powers live on."

He had to be referring to Sloane. My little sister—the one I had only learned about a few weeks ago—had just inherited all of our father's abilities, crowning her the new Angel of Death.

Then the bastard gave me a little waggle of his eyebrows before promptly disappearing, his words fading away on the gentle breeze.

Narrowing my eyes on the spot he'd just vacated, I tried my damnedest not to scream.

I was really starting to hate that man.

## 8

"That's it," I muttered as a wave of exhaustion damn near bowled me over. "I give up. What do you say we get out of here and get some sleep?"

Bishop frowned at me, seeming confused by the question. "You're quitting? That's not like you." With a swirl of black magic, he shoved the coffin back where it damn well belonged, smoothing the grass back into place. "What? Are you scared to find the big, bad demon, Adler?"

Maybe it was the exhaustion, maybe it was the weight of this place on my psyche, or *maybe* it was the way he damn well said it, but I was over his attitude for probably the rest of forever.

"You know what else isn't like me? Not sleeping for

forty-eight hours, not eating more than a single canape in six, or wearing a fucking ball gown at all. I'm so tired I can barely stand up, I'm traumatized beyond what any therapist in their right mind could handle, and I'm starving," I growled, ticking each complaint off on my fingers. "I'm allowed to rest. I'm allowed to take care of my basic fucking needs. And I'm allowed to not stay in a goddamn cemetery that gives me the creeps."

Bishop rolled his eyes. "Yes, *princess*, let's take care of you."

*Princess?*

"You know what?" I seethed. "I'm not doing this with you. I don't know what kind of bullshit you're on, but I suggest you go home"—*to the place I've never even seen*—"get some rest, and yank whatever the fuck has died out of your ass. Because all night long I've been dealing with one of your tantrums after another, and I am done."

"Oh, please." He scoffed, his eyes blazing gold. "I was just joking. You don't ha—"

"My suggestion," I warned, my voice turning real Southern real fast, "is you think real fucking hard before you finish that sentence. I don't have Daddy issues, sweetheart. I know my worth and how to be treated and this ain't fucking it. Go to *your* home. Get some rest.

Come talk to me when you've fixed your shit. You're five hundred years old, Bishop. Fucking act like it."

"Bu—"

"Nuh-uh." I cut him off, holding up a finger for him to shush. "There is not a thing you can say to me right now that will dig your ass out of this hole. Go wherever it is that you live and get your shit sorted."

Bishop's jaw clenched, his hands balling into fists as he stared at me with his golden irises. Oh, he was mad, was he? Well, I was contemplating calling Hildy and J and telling one of them to bring a shovel, so we were about on the same level.

"Fine," he ground out, "have it your way. You always do." After that blisteringly acidic parting shot, he disappeared into the darkness as though he'd been made from it.

"Fuck you, too, Bishop La Roux. Fuck. You."

Narrowing my eyes, I did the only thing I could possibly think to do. I snatched my clutch open and fished out my cell phone. I needed J. He could pick me up and... ask questions.

Bribery. I would have to go with bribery.

After three rings, my best friend in the world picked up with a groggy, "Hello? D?"

"Can you pick me up?" My plea came out a fuck of a

lot more hurt than I'd intended, the weight of Bishop's last words to me leaving a lasting sting.

"Where are you?" J asked, his voice no longer clouded with sleep. Hell, I even heard the jingling of his keys, as if he was almost out the door already.

Unable to just come out with it, I dithered, damn near throwing a mini temper tantrum as the shivers got to me. The last time I'd been in this cemetery—again, at night—it hadn't ended well. "Haunted Peak Memorial Cemetery."

*"What?"* His voice echoed down the line loud enough to rattle my eardrum, which almost made me miss the crank of his engine. "What are you doing at that cemetery, Darby?"

I sighed, pinching my brow. "How about you don't ask me any questions, and I'll forget our entire sophomore year of college when you played Celine Dion on repeat after getting dumped by Beau Copeland?"

J hissed, the mere mention of the illustrious Beau Copeland still a sore subject over a decade later. "Ow."

"Yep. I'll forget it completely and never utter his name again. Or give you shit about you confiscating our apartment sound system and performing a torture that is now outlawed by the Geneva Convention."

J's breakup had been rough. Beau was beautiful and smart and funny and love-bombed my best friend to distraction. Then he'd broken my best friend's heart in such a way that I *may* have employed Hildy to torture him just a little bit.

It served the little cheater right.

"Deal. I will not ask you a single question and pick you up at the ass crack of dawn at a cemetery you nearly died at yesterday. Especially since you have a big, strapping man who can spirit you anywhere. But it's me you call for a ride. Sure. No questions. No problem at all."

Huffing a laugh, I pivoted on a heel and pointed my feet in the direction of the cemetery's exit.

"And if you stop on the way and get me enough food to make up for the two meals I missed, I'll forget about the leech incident."

If any memory required brain bleach, it was the leech incident. J had been fooling around with his stage-five-clinger of a summer fling, and they'd gone skinny dipping in the pond behind Mr. Miller's barn. Somehow, J had gotten a leech stuck to his... *unmentionables*, and who had he called to save his ass?

Me.

The memory still made me gag.

J didn't even hesitate. "Done."

I didn't blame him. Who wanted anyone to remember your most embarrassing moment? Especially when said most embarrassing moment required peeling a leach off your dick?

"Sweet. I'm going to start walking. I can't stay here. I'll meet you on the road. I'll be the bitch in a huge ball gown."

J snorted at my sad attempt at a joke. "Sounds good. Keep your thumb on the call button and your hand on your gun, will you?" he pleaded. "I swear you're going to make me go gray."

That managed to bring a little quirk to my lips. It wasn't a smile, but it was the best I could do. "I love you, too, jerk."

"See you in five."

As I hung up, I smartly pulled my ankle piece and chambered a round. It wouldn't do a damn thing against a ghost, but if something solid wanted to attack me in the middle of the night, at least I'd be ready. But even though my eyes scanned the road for threats as I trudged in a stupid ball gown down the street, it was my mind doing the real damage.

Bishop's words lashed at me over and over again, each time opening the wound wider, deeper. By the time the headlights of J's SUV rolled over me, I was smack-dab in the middle of an epic pity party.

It took the both of us to stuff me and my dress into the back seat, but through it all, I didn't say a word—

not until after my first bite of the breakfast sandwich. As soon as the gooey melted cheese and salty sausage and fluffy egg hit my tongue, I started bawling like a freaking baby. Tears streamed down my cheeks as I shoveled food in my mouth, the hiccups from the crying nearly making me choke. I had half of the second sandwich down my gullet before J shoved a wad of napkins in my hand.

"Dear sweet mother of all that is holy. I don't care if you forget Celine Dion or Beau Copeland. Blow your nose and spill it."

But I didn't know where to start. *Wait, yes, I did.* "Do I always have to have it my way?"

J waited until he was stopped at a red light before twisting in his seat and staring at me like I was insane. "He said that?"

I couldn't do better than a shrug, which had J's cheeks pinking a little as he swiveled back to face the road. His fingers clenched the steering wheel hard enough that his knuckles turned white, but his voice was as calm as I'd ever heard it.

"Who makes sure my favorite drinks are in their fridge, or my go-to food is in their cupboard? Who does the paperwork I hate or makes sure our cases get closed properly? Who takes care of every single person they meet, taking on far more than her fair share?"

I didn't answer, but he didn't need me to because the man was on a roll.

"Who comes with me to concerts, even though you hate it? Who drives all the time so I can sleep? Who pulls pranks instead of getting people written up for procedural infractions? You give a shit about the people in your life, D. You do it in a variety of ways, and for him to leave you alone in that fucking graveyard after everything..." He shook his head. "After everything *he* put you through? The lying. The secrets. The double crosses."

J shoved down the accelerator as he took the on-ramp for the highway, his jaw clenching so hard his teeth started creaking from the pressure. "You know what this is, don't you?"

Keeping right on with my peak food consumption, I merely shrugged. I had a working theory, but I was a little too hurt to put much effort into ironing it out.

"Bet money he's mad he's not top dog anymore. Two days ago, he was a big, bad ABI agent. Now he's a nobody with no badge, no leeway, and *you* outrank *him*." J rubbed at his temple. "Remember Miles? It's just like that, only worse because you're dealing with a death mage who can't handle his girlfriend has more power than him."

J was referencing his former boyfriend, Harris Miles,

who lost his shit when J had not only gotten top grad at the academy but beat his record on the obstacle course. Miles had thrown the mother of all hissy fits and broken up with him the same day. Damn near ruined J's graduation he was so sad.

"What a little bitch," J muttered. "He's probably worried your dick's bigger than his."

I snorted, nearly choking on my last sandwich. Struggling to breathe, I sucked back soda, allowing the fire of the carbonation to clear my throat. "I don't have a dick, you asshole," I croaked. "And don't make me laugh. I can't afford to lose this food. It's the first time I've been able to sit down and eat in like two days. I'm wasting away over here."

"That man let you miss a meal?" He took his eyes off the road to shoot me a glare in the rearview mirror. "And you let him?"

Again, with the shrugging. I *had* been a little busy.

"You need a good night's rest and to get the hell out of that damn dress."

"Tell me about it," I groused, settling further into my seat as lethargy pulled at my limbs. "If I never see a skirt again, it'll be too soon."

Before my eyes could close, though, J asked a question that had me waking all the way up. "Do you really love him?"

Staring at the ceiling of his car, I thought about it for a second, but J didn't even let me formulate an answer.

"Because I've been thinking about it, and I have to wonder if you're with him by default," he said, dropping a verbal bomb onto my whole life. "I wasn't there for you when you needed me, and he was—taking up for you with all that arcane shit."

I swallowed, tears clogging my throat, but I couldn't say anything.

"So do you love him, or is it just because he was there for you? Do you love him, or are you just grateful he brought Killian back? Do you love him, or is he just the first man you allowed yourself to get close to?"

J never did get an answer, my jaw too clenched to say a word. But luckily, the tears that fell down my face were silent.

## 9

The lurch of J's car stopping had me startling awake. Fortunately, I only had a blade in my hand, so at least no one got shot when I lifted off the seat as if someone had pressed the eject button.

"Are you sure you want to stay here?" J asked, staring at the giant Victorian with a heavy dose of skepticism. "You know you could stay in my guest room. Hell, even Cap would put you up if you didn't—"

Now that I had a hold on myself, I put a hand up to stop J's offer. "There are three agents in that house. Three. I'm fine. Plus, all my clothes are here."

Yeah, my protest was lame, but I didn't want to impose on any of them. Plus, if shit went down, having what remained of my family close would only make the pit of unease in my belly worse. It was better if I didn't bring my bullshit to J's doorstep—at least until Jimmy made him a necklace like mine.

J seemed to see through my bullshit. "Sure. And it has nothing to do with your house blowing up and my weak human status."

"You aren't weak," I protested, wishing he understood. And he wasn't. But he was fragile, and I'd been trying to keep his dumbass out of this shit for a hot minute. "Now let me get some rest, you turd, and call me tomorrow, yeah?"

J flipped his visor down at the coming sunrise, a yawn cracking his jaw. "It *is* tomorrow. I'll call you later, deal?"

"Deal. Now help me out of this car and give me a hug. Also, if you see Sarina before I do, inform her that I am burning this dress the first chance I get."

Snorting, he peeled himself from the driver seat before peeling me from the back, the level of tulle and underskirt making the task damn near impossible. Hell, if I made it through the door of the house it would be a miracle.

J gave me one of his patented hugs, the embrace almost as awesome as my dad's had been. It was warm and soft and held just the tiniest bit of nostalgia that made me miss my childhood.

"Love you, D."

Playfully, I lightly punched him in the gut. "Love you, too, weirdo. Now call Jimmy so he can make sure you stay awake."

"Will do," he said, his phone already in his hand as he restarted his car.

Dutifully, he waited until I was almost in the house before driving away, and I was in the relative safety of the doorway before a ghost nearly scared the absolute shit out of me.

"Miss Darby?" a small voice called, the sight of the child creeping me all the way out.

Swallowing, I got my body under control enough to respond.

"Hello, Linus," I murmured, greeting Acker's ghostly brother who was sitting in the rocker on the front porch. He was desperately trying to move the chair but seemed unable to budge the wood.

I was still unclear on the details, but from what I gathered, Acker had accidentally killed his brother when they were seven, his nature too out of control at that age to be stopped. Agent Acker had since had his powers bound, but that didn't stop him from regretting what he'd done.

To help out, I nudged the rocker, letting it move for the boy. "You okay?"

Typically, I loathed child ghosts. The loss of a child—

even though it wasn't my own—stung in a way that always brought a weight to my chest. You know, when they weren't scaring the ever-loving shit out of me, that was.

Linus shrugged, his little shoulders lifting and dropping like an anvil. "I miss Ambrose. He doesn't come outside much, and now that he knows I'm here…"

"You want me to talk to him for you?" I offered. "He might come out and spend some time with you if I ask."

The boy fiddled with his fingers. "I just want to play with him. I miss watching him work. He wouldn't talk too much, but sometimes, he'd say things in his sleep. It was nice. Like I was almost being seen."

Yup. Child ghosts were the worst. I was pretty sure I was on track to solid dehydration from the sheer number of tears that threatened to fall.

"Do you think maybe it's time to move on? I've heard Elysium is nice."

Linus ducked his head, his shoulders scrunching up by his ears. "Oh, I won't go there."

Kneeling in this dress was ridiculous, but I managed it to look Linus in the eye. "Why not, sweetheart? You seem like a good soul. I doubt there was—"

Linus flickered, and then he was no longer in the chair but in the yard. "I did bad things. Bad," he insisted, his form flashing like Hildy's had. The absolute last thing I wanted was to make this kid turn. "I'll go right to Hell if you make me go."

Getting to my feet, I held up both hands in the universal sign of surrender. "Okay, Linus. I won't make you go. And I'll talk to Ambrose. Deal? Maybe he'll come talk to you in the garden."

He twisted the toe of his boot in the grass as he peered up at me from underneath his lashes. "You think he would?"

I swear this boy would break my heart. "Won't know until I ask him, now, will I?"

That seemed to brighten the boy and he faded from sight, probably going to the backyard to wait. Bone-tired, I opened the front door and trudged up the stairs, ready to get the hell out of this dress and get some sleep.

It took far more work getting out of the damn thing by myself than I'd have liked, but soon I was divested of the dress from Hell. I washed the makeup off my face, thankful that at least came off easy enough, and I gave up on trying to remove the necklace Jimmy had made. The clasp was too much for me after too little sleep. I decided "Screw it" before crawling into bed.

A bed that still smelled of Bishop.

Irritated, I snatched his pillow and threw it across

the room. The memory of his twisted expression was there to stay, however, so were J's words.

*Sleep. I need sleep.*

Settling in, I brought the covers over my shoulder and did my best to doze off.

*Yes, princess, let's take care of you.*

*Have it your way. You always do.*

*Do you love him, or is he just the first man you allowed yourself to get close to?*

A growl worked its way up my throat as I kicked the duvet off my legs. This was utter and complete bullshit. I'd been up far too long, and I was due a good night's rest. Grumbling, I heaved myself out of bed, naturally tripping over Bishop's pillow and damn near face-planting on the floor.

Snatching up the pillow, I may or may not have beaten the poor thing against the bed several times before I launched it across the room. Grumbling, I shoved my feet into slippers and stuffed my arms into a robe, tying the knot so tight it creaked.

Fuck it. If I couldn't have sleep, I would mainline coffee until I had a psychotic break. Well, that and figure out what Azrael had to do with putting Aemon in his cage.

*Okay, Sloane, I need information, so if you could pause your death-dealing duties and come have a cup of coffee with me, that'd be great.*

I made my way to the kitchen, blessing whoever made the last pot as soon as I saw the liquid gold, and sent an extra one for the person responsible for making sure it was fresh, hot, and... was that French Roast? Hell, I almost giggled when I found the five bottles of cinnamon roll flavored creamer in the fridge.

Pouring two mugs, I passed one off to my sister, the relief of her actually being here easing a hurt place in my chest that I hadn't realized I'd had.

Sloane's hair was braided in a tail over her shoulder —her hair much longer than it'd been when I'd seen it last. The same was the glow to her skin that told of her otherworldly lineage. Dressed in jeans and a skull and crossbones T-shirt, I figured all she was missing was the scythe and she'd be the picture of Death.

She gratefully took the mug from me, her smile devious. "So," she began before taking a sip, "how's Deimos?"

Unlike with the man in question, I did not fight the urge to flip her off. "Would it have killed you to give me a little heads-up? Oh, that's right, you're already dead." I yanked out a barstool and settled in. "Verbally sparring with the God of Torment is not my idea of a good time, you know. Neither is being possessed by his son."

Sloane winced as she took the seat next to me. "Yeah... Sorry about that. If I could have told you, I would have. As shitty as it was, it happened like it was supposed to."

I couldn't stop my eyes from rolling. "Every once in a while, flip off Fate for me, will ya?"

She snorted into her mug. "Trust me. She did you a solid. I saw the alternatives. That was the best-case scenario."

My mug hit the stone with a *thunk*. "You mean it could have been *worse*?"

Worse than being almost ripped in half and suffocated?

Worse than Bishop making a deal with my life on the line?

Worse than those witches dying?

"Yes, to all of the above," she muttered, nodding as she read my thoughts. Being around Sarina all the time, I was used to it, but it still sucked.

"Just trust me on this. It would have been a long-lasting shitstorm that would have eventually led to your ultimate end. No part of it was good, so I left you to it. Had I interfered?" She shuddered, her violet eyes flashing. "*No bueno*."

I snagged my cup from the counter. "Thanks for not

butting in, I guess? Any chance of an assist with Deimos in the cards for me?"

Sloane winced again—an expression I was seriously starting to hate—and waggled her hand at me. "I can't *tell* you, but I suppose showing you the backstory can't hurt."

"The backstory? And show me?" I slugged back a piping-hot mouthful of the glorious French roast. "Please tell me this isn't going to suck."

She squinted as if she was trying to figure out how to explain it. "When Azrael gave me what remained of his power, he also gave me a fair bit of information, along with the wings."

I chuckled, remembering the last time I'd seen her. She hadn't quite figured out how to put them away at the time, but the glorious black wings were nowhere to be seen. "Nice to see you figured out how to hide them. I doubt they'd fit in the kitchen."

"Right? Well, I think I know a way to show you like he did me—you know without all the growing of wings and power transfer shit."

My skepticism was ripe. "You *think*?"

She held up a hand and wiggled her fingers at me. "I'm ninety-four-point-three percent sure I won't make you grow feathers."

Thinking about it for maybe a second, I shrugged. Honestly, after the night I'd had, growing wings would be the absolute least of my problems. And I'd experienced some of Azrael's memories before. Granted, they hadn't been a picnic, but I figured it couldn't be any worse than seeing my whole world falling apart, now, could it?

I gave her my hand, allowing our palms to touch, and instantly, my mind was bombarded by a vision. The familiar taste of Azrael's memories flooded my mind, only this time, the cadence of his voice, of his kindness with the dead, hurt in a way I couldn't express.

*The young man seemed confused as I reached for him. I, too, was rather puzzled. He was not on my list. In fact, this particular man wasn't supposed to die for another twenty-eight years. He was supposed to have children, grandchildren. He was supposed to invent a new way to fire clay, so his pottery was stronger. His son was supposed to give this knowledge away for free, allowing other potters to advance.*

*Dragging my gaze from the soul that shouldn't be here, I stared at the field of them waiting for me. None of them were on my list—not one in this sea of hundreds. Clenching the man's hand tighter, I pulled the memory of his death from him, the dark magic of his demise giving me only a single name if not a face.*

*Nero.*

．  ．  ．

*"What is it, Azrael. Can't you see I'm busy?" Deimos grumbled, ready to get back to his work.*

*He smiled proudly at the rapist who was slowly rotating on a spit over a mound of vipers. Every time the soul's flank got within reach, one of the snakes would strike, pumping venom into a body that never died. The trick was that Deimos oversaw the rotations, and he would slow them ever so slightly so the soul never knew when the next strike would come. Fitting, since the women he'd defiled and murdered never knew when he would strike, either.*

*When the God of Torment got tired of this specific torture, he would think up a new and inventive one to replace it.*

*He always did.*

*"Get unbusy. We have a problem." It was bad enough I had to inform him that one of his demons had made a bad deal, but even worse that the demon in question was his own son.*

*"Fine," he relented, passing off his duties to a lower demon. "Don't stop until he starts screaming," Deimos instructed. "And when he does, add the ants."*

*The demon nodded vigorously, a devious smile pulling at her lips.*

*"What problem could possibly be big enough for you to come down here?" Deimos spread his arms wide, gesturing at the pit at large. "Doesn't your kind prefer to stay topside?"*

*Yes, I did prefer to stay out of Tartarus. The screams were inherently unpleasant.*

*"A deal has been struck," I began, only to be cut off by the impatient god.*

*"Deals are struck every day," Deimos muttered, conjuring an apple from thin air and biting into it. "Please tell me you haven't ruined my fun over a simple deal," he complained around the fruit.*

*"Not a simple deal. A deal big enough to disrupt Fate." My hissing did nothing to convey the gravity of the situation since Deimos pretended to clutch his heart and dramatically fall over.*

*"That woman needs to be disrupted. She and her sisters. A bunch of whiney sticks in the mud, the lot of them."*

*Pinching my brow, I growled, "This is serious, you idiot. Thousands of humans are dying far earlier than their time. Not one or two. Thousands. Humans that were meant to have children. That were meant to invent things. That were meant to change the world. The ripple this has caused will be felt until the end of time."*

*Deimos finally stopped chewing. "All this from one deal?"*

*"It was a powerful deal—one that could have only been made from the royal line."*

*Rage ignited behind the god's eyes. "Aemon."*

*He'd supplied the culprit before I could, which had me breathing a sigh of relief. Aemon had always been his favorite, his protégé. This was not a grievance I'd ever wanted to bring to his table.*

*"Yes. And the deal was made with a human, a Roman soldier by the name of Nero. Funnily enough, he's a general now, leading an army into a war that shouldn't occur for another four hundred years."*

*Deimos' face almost instantly turned a worrying shade of purple before all expression wiped clean from his features. "You have my attention and assistance. What shall we do about this?"*

*In the end, it took both of us to put Aemon down, and I made a promise to deal with Nero when he passed.*

*Deimos seemed to think the matter was resolved, but me?*

*I had a feeling the Prince of Hell would be a far sight worse to deal with if he finally broke free.*

"That's it," Sloane announced as she yanked me out of the shared vision. "This is all I can show you."

Confused, I latched onto her sleeve. "Hold up. Can't you tell me how Azrael dealt with Nero when he died? That is a memory I would love to watch. Did you see how many innocent people he—"

"Can't." Sloane shrugged as she rested her chin on her fist, her other hand reaching for a plate of cookies I hadn't noticed. She bit into the cookie, and with a mouthful of food, she said, "He's not dead."

"But... that would make him hella old. Older than dirt old. He'd have to be a vampire." I arched a brow at my sister, praying she wasn't about to confirm my suspicions. "Right?"

And if he was a vampire and still alive, then I had an idea of where Aemon would go next. Hell, if I'd been imprisoned for a couple millennia after a deal went south, revenge would be at the top of my list.

Sloane shot me a devious grin, revealing a hint of fang. "A Roman soldier turned vampire," she mused, tapping her chin with her index finger. "If only you knew a vampire turned during Roman times..."

My shoulders wilted, and I thumped my head on the counter.

*Ingrid.*

## 10

"**I**s she okay?" a timid voice asked as I continued to thump my head against the stone counter. "I know she's special and all, but brain damage is a thing."

Rotating my head on the cool stone, I glared at Tobin with enough heat that he stumbled back a step, knocking into Yazzie. "Did you make the coffee?"

Frowning, Tobin ran a hand through his mess of black curls. "Maybe. That depends on if you liked it or not."

Lifting my head, I smiled. "I rescind my glare then. You are a prince among men, and don't let anyone tell you any different."

The agents shared a puzzled glance before the pair of them eyed me with suspicion, but it was Yazzie who called me on it. "Why do I feel like this is a precursor to a task neither of us is going to like?"

Sloane snorted, taking a sip of her coffee. "Probably because you have good survival instincts?"

Like the totally with-it and completely adult big sister I was, I stuck my tongue out at her. "Guys, this is my sister, Sloane—also known as the Angel of Death." I gestured to the agents who seemed ready to bolt from the room at any moment. "This is Agent Jensen Yazzie and Aldrich Tobin. Acker is around here somewhere."

Sloane's smile was wide as ever, her fangs peeking out just a little as a wave of sheer menace came wafting off of her. "Is that the one you kneed in the nose, or was it one of these two?"

"It was a misunderstanding. You know how people can be about death," I said, bugging my eyes out at her. She was going to give the agents a heart attack. "Speaking of Acker, I need a favor. Wait in the garden for me?"

*And quit scaring the agents, you turd. If they leave, I'll have to do all my own scut work, and you know how much I hate that.*

Sloane got up, stealing another cookie as she went. "Nice to meet you, boys," she said around the confection. "I'll be seeing you around," she teased, sauntering out the back door to the garden.

*Not helpful,* I thought in her direction as both Yazzie

and Tobin adhered themselves to the kitchen walls to avoid touching my sister as she passed.

"She's not contagious, you know," I chided the pair of them, shaking my head. "She doesn't actually kill people. Well, not unless you piss her off."

Tobin looked ready to faint, so I grabbed a cookie and stuffed it in his hand. "Focus, will you? I need your help."

Nibbling on the treat, he seemed to perk up. "What do you need?"

"For you to dig up absolutely everything you have on an ancient vampire named Nero. Everything. What he looks like, pictures if you've got them, origins, maker, all the way down to his goddamn shoe size. I want to know who he's bled and bedded, everyone he's fucked up or fucked over, and I need it pronto."

A change came over Tobin's face as if he were peeling back a mask. Gone was the scared little boy who I could snap like a twig, and here was a man who had just been given carte blanche to do his favorite thing in the entire world. His eyes lit up like Christmas as he rubbed his hands together, not realizing he was crumbling his cookie to dust as he did so.

"*Everything?*" He breathed like I was talking dirty to him. Hell, I probably was.

"Break rules if you have to. If I have to find a demon,

the man whose deal put him in the ground is the first place I'm gonna look. Be sneaky, be devious, and for fuck's sake, don't get caught. Deal?"

Tobin nodded vigorously. "I'll have a preliminary report to you in no time."

The agent stuffed what was left of his cookie in his mouth and beat feet out of the kitchen, practically leaving a jet trail in his wake.

Yazzie shook his head as he poured himself a cup of coffee. "You just gave that boy the gift of a lifetime. No one ever lets him go nuts. It's always 'can you fix my computer' and 'set up the surveillance equipment' shit. You realize he's going to worship you now, right?"

"But isn't research part of his job? Why wouldn't I get him to do that shit? I sure as hell don't want to. And he's happy about getting scut work? All the better." I thought about that statement for a second. "What is it *you* like to do?"

Yazzie lifted one shoulder as he sipped his black coffee. "Keeping my ear out for trouble. Researching shifter movements. Making sure no one is stepping out of line."

A wave of relief washed over me. Maybe this Warden shit would work out. "Then that's what I need you to do. Talking to the alpha last night did not go as I planned—not that I had a real plan—but you get the idea. LeBlanc never planned for me to walk out of there, and he damn sure didn't plan on me winning that challenge. I expect some retaliation—especially since I made him look like a little bitch in front of his pack."

Yazzie took my former seat at the bar, proceeding to thump his head on the counter, much as I had. "I told you not to go there."

"Yeah, well, not going would have meant I wasn't doing my job, so it wasn't like I could sit there with my thumb up my ass and pray they didn't kill anyone else. You didn't see it. That girl was unstable."

"Oh, I saw. Delivering her and her brothers to the ABI was a swell experience. She woke up mid-transfer and nearly took out an agent's eye. I doubt she'll make it to her tribunal."

Cringing, I refilled his mug, praying that was enough of a goodwill gesture to get him onboard. "Just keep an ear out."

Yazzie snorted as he pulled out his phone, showing me the screen. "One step ahead of you, boss."

I was confused for about a millisecond before I realized what I was looking at. The screen was filled with tiny squares, each one with surveillance footage of the LeBlanc compound.

*"Oh, I can't go in. It's too dangerous,"* I grumbled,

imitating Yazzie's deep voice. "You dirty, underhanded, sneaky sneak. I love it."

His smile was radiant from the praise. "I'm not an idiot. But those wolves they use as sentries sure are. All it took was staying downwind, and they were oblivious."

"You're a damn genius, is what you are. Keep me posted, will you?"

Moving toward the back door, I snagged the last cookie from the plate right out from under Yazzie's fingers. Yes, I was poking a bear—literally—but food was food. He let out a teensy little growl of warning, but I was already out the door with the relative safety of my little sister as backup.

Sloane lounged on a teak patio chair, staring at a little boy pretending to play in the dirt.

*Why does he think he's going to Hell? He's just a little boy,* I said inside my head so as to not scare the child. Linus was skittish at best, and if he knew who Sloane was, he'd bolt the first chance he got.

*He accidentally killed his baby sister. Their parents didn't know the Mormo gene passed to the boys. They allowed them to be too close to the baby, thinking it was okay since the children were male. He couldn't control his nature. It's why Ambrose killed him. It's no one's fault. It just is.*

Someone was cutting onions somewhere in the vicinity, or I had allergies or something. Or the thought of a turn of fate that shitty made me want to curl up and bawl my eyes out. You know, whatever. It took everything I had left in the tank to not snatch that poor boy up and hug him.

*You wouldn't take him to Tartarus, would you? For an accident?*

Sloane rotated in her seat to stare me down. There was enough heat in that expression to have me taking a step back. Holding my hands up in surrender, I shrugged. "I had to ask. But knowing the coast is clear, do you think you could talk to him? Let him know that he doesn't have to be scared to pass. That if he wanted to go play with the kids in Elysium, he could?"

Her piercing gaze left me so she could inspect Linus. "Yeah," she huffed. "I can do that."

"Hey, Linus," I called. "Come meet someone."

The little boy zoomed closer, staring at Sloane like she was the prettiest girl he'd ever seen. He didn't get too close, though, my warning of touching people still burned in his brain. "She looks like you, Miss Darby. All shiny and glowing. Like a jewel in the river."

"That's because I'm Darby's sister," she answered, her voice softer than I'd ever heard it as she rose from her seat and approached the boy.

Linus took a step back, a dash of apprehension on his brow. "If I touch you, will I go to the bad place, too?"

Sloane smiled as she bumped him with her hip. "Nope. But that's because you weren't going to the bad place, anyway."

His little boy face screwed up like he didn't believe her. "How do you know?"

"It's my job, kid." She knelt down to look him in the eye. "Do you know who our dad was?" At his shaking head, she continued, "He was the Angel of Death—he took people who died to their afterlife. Now that my dad is dead, I do his job. So if you were going to Hell, I'd know."

Hope bloomed on his face for a moment before his gaze shifted to the door behind me. "But I'd leave Ambrose behind."

"True," Sloane nodded, "but I think he'd want you to rest, don't you?" She gently grasped his hand and wiggled his arm so he'd look at her. "But you don't have to come with me right now. Only when you're ready, okay?"

Shimmering tears filled Linus' eyes. "You sure I'm not..." He trailed off, not daring to finish that sentence, and I had to grit my teeth to not lose it.

"I'm sure," she whispered. "I promise you that Elysium is waiting for you whenever you're ready." Then she winked, waved, and disappeared as if she had never been there at all. Instantly, I felt the loss, wishing I'd gotten to hug her before she left.

Linus' smile, though, made it a little better. "You going, too?"

After that gut-punch? Abso-fucking-lutely. "I'll still talk to Ambrose for you when I see him, okay?"

He nodded. "Thanks, Miss Darby. I do feel better now."

"I'm glad, kid," I muttered, heading back into the house.

And I was.

Until I remembered what I had to do next.

Staring at the carcass of the Dubois cathedral, I seriously contemplated my life choices. After interrupting Tobin's Nero research to ask for another favor, I now had the location of my illustrious yet tiny friend, and I was not happy about it.

According to Tobin, Ingrid was in this burned-out wreck of a building, and if I wanted to talk to her, I'd have to go in there. I'd have to risk my life entering a completely unsafe structure all because some demon's daddy wanted to make my life a living hell.

Well, that and Ingrid wasn't answering her fucking phone.

As much as Ing had backed me up over the years, there was no reality where I wouldn't charge through a highly unsafe building to go get her tiny ass, but...

I really didn't want to.

Pouting, I beeped the locks on the Jeep and proceeded to have an utter and complete hissy fit as I headed into the building. A structure this size should still be smoldering, and I was starting to rethink my T-shirt and jeans combo. At the very least, I was smart enough to slap boots on my feet, a gun on my hip, and enough blades to start a war, but it still felt like too little coverage. Reaching inside my bag, I snagged my leather jacket and shoved my arms into the sleeves, despite the heat.

I'd take a little sweat over tetanus any day.

Instead of entering through the front door—which was blocked by two struts that had snapped in half—I climbed through a broken side window, thankful I'd been with-it enough to put the damn jacket on. Part of the spire had collapsed into the gallery, the two-hundred-year-old hallmark of the cathedral nothing more than rubble as it littered the once-beautiful structure.

Picking my way through the detritus, I headed for the catacombs underneath the former church. I officially hated this part of Ingrid's home. Having only been here twice, I was not excited for this to be round three.

The stone tunnels reminded me of Simon's entrance to the Underworld, the rock damp and grimy, even though I knew someone cleaned the place daily—or at least they used to.

*How is living in a cave worse than this, exactly?*

My boots echoed as I clomped through the first tunnel—on purpose—and I turned right at the second fork, praying I was going the right way. I did not want to ever sneak up on Ingrid, but when I finally recognized where I was and knocked on her door, it didn't seem to matter how loud I'd been. My tiny friend was engrossed in reading a slip of parchment as she nervously nibbled on her thumbnail.

"If I were a snake," I began, startling the shit out of her, "I would have bit you ten times over by now. What the fuck, Ingrid?"

Eyes flashing, teeth bared, she nearly attacked before she recognized me. "Are you out of your mind? I could have killed you. What are you doing here? Can't you see this place is dangerous?"

Snorting, I threw my hands out wide. "If you would answer your fucking phone, I wouldn't have to worry about your ass and track you down. What are you doing here, you fucking weirdo?"

It was bad enough her room looked like a bad vampire movie had just thrown up on it with its black satin sheets and stark décor, but coupled with the fact that it was in a literal catacomb under a cathedral? All of it gave me the creeps. I would not be here if I wasn't worried.

"Inspecting the damage and making sure those wolves didn't actually get more than witch blood on their hands. We didn't exactly have a chance to clear out of here with a ton of time to spare."

I had to give her that. Had Sarina not given us a heads-up, the Dubois nest would have been toast. And even though we won against Essex's lackeys, the safety of this place was long gone.

And that had been before a trio of wolves decided to set the place on fire.

"You think they got anything?" The LeBlanc pack was large, devious, and a significant pain in my ass. If they were starting shit, this would be the place they'd do it.

Ingrid scanned the room, her face pensive. "I don't know. It's too hard to tell. It does make me wish we would have done more than just kick them out of Tennessee, though. No good deed goes unpunished, right?"

I knew the feeling.

"But you needed me," she muttered. "What had you trekking all the way down here to your favorite place in the world?"

Wincing, I rested a shoulder on the doorframe. "I need information and maybe an in with someone you might know. He made a deal with Aemon a few millennia ago for power, and I think the demon might want to find him." Considering he was an awful murderer, conqueror, and an all-around horrible person, it just figured that the bastard would be looking for the vamp.

Ingrid waved her hand for me to continue.

"He used to be a Roman soldier, but I think he might be a vamp to have survived this long. His name is Nero. Have you ever heard of him?"

Ingrid's eyes flashed crimson as her already-pale face turned ashen. Fangs descended, expression blank, she stalked closer to me as her small hands balled into fists.

"Where," she growled, her voice a guttural nightmare, "did you hear that name?"

## 11

There were a ton of beings I did not want to piss off since I valued breathing.

Ingrid Dubois was one of them.

Backing away slowly, I held my hands up in surrender. I was doing my best to not anger the older-than-dirt apex predator that could drink me down in three seconds flat. "As I said, he's the man Aemon might be looking for. I need to find Aemon and have no idea where to start, but the reason he got put down is still breathing, so—"

"So, nothing," she spat, her body practically vibrating as she stalked closer. "No good ever comes from saying that name. No good comes from finding him. No—" She shook her head, the violent jerks of her chin making my heart sink down into my toes. "No."

"Are you sure, child?" a familiar voice purred from behind, and it took everything in me not to jump three feet in the air. Deimos stood much like I had a moment ago, the shoulder of his crisp suit resting against the gritty stone wall. "You seem so adamant, but you don't yet know why we want your maker."

*Her maker?* My heart fell to my feet as I studied my friend—her childlike features, her perfectly plaited hair, her schoolgirl uniform. The man who'd murdered so many had made her into a vampire?

*No wonder she's freaking out.*

A still-vamped Ingrid shuffled backward, nearly knocking into a dressing table before she righted herself.

"What," I barked, moving my body so I was in between them, "do I have a tracker on my ass or something?"

The God of Torment shot me an evil smile that reminded me of his son's. "In a manner of speaking. Why don't you formally introduce me to your little friend? You were so rude the last time."

Rolling my eyes, I unenthusiastically gestured to him. "Ingrid Dubois, this is the God of Torment, Deimos. Deimos, this is Ingrid Dubois. Happy?"

"Much." Deimos directed his attention to Ingrid, making the vamp shudder. "Considering who Nero is to you, I figured you would be begging to help us." He narrowed his gaze, seeming to peer inside her mind. "But I guess not."

"Obviously," I muttered, approaching Ingrid with caution. Gently, I dropped a hand to her shoulder so she'd look at me instead of the god who was most likely playing with her like a toy. "If Ing says Nero's bad news and we don't want to fool with him, I believe her. I'm just going to have to find another way to get to Aemon."

And I would. Sure, Nero needed to go down, but I had a sister who could do that job. Aemon was my goal. Not Nero. And if this was causing Ing to freak to this level? I wanted no part of any of it.

"Oh, she'll help," Deimos muttered breezily, his smile not dropping an inch.

"No," Ingrid argued, "*she* won't. I don't know you, and I don't want to. And D, I love you, but this would burn through every favor and boon you could earn until the end of time. There is nothing I owe you worth..." Ingrid shook her head, her body shuddering violently. "No."

She shrugged my hand off her shoulder and skirted the room, giving Deimos and me a wide berth. Just as she was nearly out of the room, Deimos' words stopped her cold.

"What if I told you that when we find Nero, we'll kill him in addition to capturing my son? What if I told you that this is exactly what Aemon plans to do—kill the man who swindled him out of the last two millennia? All we need is to make sure we have Aemon and Nero in the same place at the same time."

Ingrid thawed just enough to glare at the god, an expression that had me wishing I was anywhere else. "You could have fucking led with that, instead of making me relive two thousand years of fear and memories. But I suppose you wouldn't be the God of Torment without the torture bit, now, would you?" She shook her head and tacked on, "Asshole."

Deimos' form flickered just a bit, his smile stretching just a touch too wide, showing far too many teeth to fit in a standard-sized mouth. "Aemon won't just want his life. He'll want his soul, too. He will most likely rip it to shreds as he drags that man all the way down to Tartarus where he belongs. My son has been waiting two millennia to exact his payment and for being stuck in a box. Well, I can't say I blame him."

She seemed to internally deliberate for a while, studying Deimos as she found an upended chair and righted it. "You know who he is and what he's done. Yes?"

Ingrid had never spoken of her sire, and given the turning process for vamps, I assumed her maker had been younger like she'd been when he was turned. Or at least that's what I'd hoped. Knowing what I did now and her reaction to the mere mention of his name, I had a feeling my small friend had endured far more than she ever let on.

"I do," Deimos agreed, his macabre smile growing wider, as if he were contemplating just what he had planned for the ancient vamp. "I know everything." He tapped his temple. "Every sin, every monstrous thing, all the facets of your turning. I can see it."

Ingrid's hold on the chair grew tight enough that the wood splintered under her fingers. "Get out of my head."

Deimos shrugged, his face losing some of its more frightening qualities. "Fine. But I'm not the only one who has rooted around in there. I have a feeling I know how Aemon learned Nero was still alive." He inspected his perfectly buffed fingernails. "Mariana O'Shea set this all into motion. Putting that portal in the one place she shouldn't, setting off a domino effect that allowed my son to go free."

Ingrid's face paled once more as she kicked the remnants of the chair away from her. "The cemetery. He was there, rooting inside my mind. Wasn't he?"

"That he was," Deimos answered, his expression now bored. "All it took was that little glimpse of your maker, and he formulated a plan. A rather crude one, but a plan, nevertheless. Then it was a one-two hop into your friend, and here we are."

It just figured that Mariana's treachery would cause this mess. One last "fuck you" to deal with, even though her soul was nothing more than ash. It made me wish I'd let Azrael take her to Tartarus so at least someone could be roasting her over a spit or something.

There were a lot of wrong choices made that day—primarily by me—and I hated that jumping through that portal was another on the list.

"Super," I muttered. "Thanks for boiling it down to being my fault."

"To know is to be human. To blame, however, is *divine*." He gave us both a little finger wave. "Now that you're on board, I'll be seeing you around. I'll fetch you when it's time for your part."

*Part? What part?*

But the damn man was gone before I could get an answer. I had a sinking feeling in my gut that his plan was to use Ingrid as bait. I turned back to Ingrid—to say what, I didn't know—but that bitch was gone, too, leaving me to find my way out of this creepy fucking catacomb on my own.

*Great.* Just what I wanted after nearly forty-eight hours of too little sleep, too little food, and a major fight with Bishop...

*Yes, princess, let's take care of you.*

*Have it your way. You always do.*

*Do you love him, or is he just the first man you allowed yourself to get close to?*

Shit. Every part of that argument still stung, and none of it made any sense. A few days ago, he was ready and willing to back me up. Today—or rather yesterday—he was one second away from a temper tantrum at every turn.

Aemon's burn on my chest ached, and I absently rubbed at the spot as I scanned the stark room. I had half a mind to barricade the door and curl up on the bed —satin sheets, probable bloodstains, and all. But I wouldn't get sleep there, not really. Just like I wouldn't at the Warden house. And it wasn't because I wasn't tired.

More it was the safety that had been robbed from me. Dad was gone. Azrael, too. And Bishop? Who knew if we could mend what was broken in us? Him pulling a one-eighty this soon after the big "L" was said, though? It made me wonder what else he was hiding—if he loved me at all, or if he was just using me.

He was out of the ABI now—something he'd wanted for five hundred years. And I hated that I couldn't trust that he wanted me for me. Because right now, I felt like a bridge for him to get out from under the ABI's thumb, and now that he'd gotten what he wanted, he didn't have to be with me anymore.

*Maybe he's too much of a coward to do the ending himself.*

That thought had a different pain settling into the stupid organ under my ribs.

*Is this who he really is? Is he really the bastard and not the savior?*

Swallowing down the lump in my throat, I picked my way back through the catacomb. Managing only to get lost once, I trudged past the rubble of the half-collapsed building, climbed back out the side window, and finally into the fresh morning air.

As soon as the light hit me, I practically hissed, the brightness making me just that much more worn out. Every minute of the forty-eight hours I'd been awake weighed on me as I slogged back to my Jeep. Fumbling with the stupid keys in my bag, I beeped the locks and seriously contemplated sleeping in my car.

Thinking better of it, I peeled off my bag and jacket, tossing them in the back of the Jeep. Then I yanked my phone out of my back pocket as I slid into the driver seat. For about a minute, I contemplated calling Bishop and telling him I couldn't do this shit anymore.

Well, I did right up until I remembered I didn't have the bastard's phone number.

How was this even possible? How had we gone all

the way to the "I love you" stage without exchanging fucking phone numbers? And where did he live? I'd never been to his home. Hell, I didn't even know if he lived in this state. With his shade jumping skills, he could live anywhere.

*And how in the blue fuck did I not realize this was a huge red flag just waving in my face?*

Had my life been that much of a shitshow I was that freaking colorblind? Was I that lonely, that desperate to have someone love me, that I just blithely walked past every warning in the damn book?

Shame ripped through me as I dropped the phone into the now-blurry cupholder, idiotic tears filling my eyes.

I was the dumbest dumb bitch to walk the fucking earth.

Covering my eyes, I let those stupid tears fall. If I had to cry, this was the last safe space I had left. My house was fucked, the Warden house was full of people I didn't know, and going to my childhood home seemed like something I just couldn't do. I was adrift with no anchor and no port, and every tear felt like a failure.

"Please tell me you aren't crying over your lover boy," a familiar silky voice said from far, far too close. "I'm not sure he's worth the trouble."

Slowly—oh, so slowly—I raised my head, turning it

toward what I hoped was a hallucination from too little sleep. Hell, I'd take a psychotic break at this point.

But I had a feeling the demon in my passenger seat was very, very real.

"Hello, Aemon."

## 12

W ell, if this was my end, at least I closed out my time on this earth on a high note.

I mean, I was in the process of breaking up with my first boyfriend in five years, both my dads had died on me, and my mom turned out to be an evil she-beast from the depths of Satan's anus. Add on the pissed-off ghouls, cranky witches, a wolf pack at the tipping point, and an ABI director desperate for my head, and well, I was just bowling strikes, wasn't I?

Now the demon who'd possessed me just twenty-four hours ago was waltzing back into my life like he didn't have a care in the world. I must have taken a dump on Fate's lawn in a past life.

"Of course you're here." I chuckled mirthlessly,

letting my head fall back on the headrest. "Why not? Your dad just pops in whenever he wants to. Why not you, too? What? You pissed my father helped put you down, and now you want revenge? Is that it?"

A smile bloomed across Aemon's face as he studied me. He was likely contemplating just which torture he wanted to implement first. At this point, I was so tired I just didn't care. If he wanted to kill me, he could go right on ahead and do it. What was I going to be able to do about it?

Not a damn thing, that's what.

His crystalline blue eyes glittered as his smile widened, a peek of a double set of fangs sneaking out from under his lip. Much like Sloane and Azrael, the twin razor-sharp incisors made my belly go into a free fall.

Yep, this was it. He would rip out my throat or slice me to ribbons or *something*. And that would be it.

Closing my eyes to the pretty package that was the Prince of Hell, I waited for my end. You know that saying about getting sleep when you were dead? Well, I fucking well hoped so because this level of insomnia was for the birds.

But instead of the blow I'd expected, the air shifted as the leather seat under his ass creaked a bit. Cracking an eyelid, I got an eyeful of Aemon, his face way too close to mine for comfort. Both my eyes popped wide as I plastered myself to the driver's side door.

"Why would you think my quarrel with Azrael would transfer to you? Did you put me in that box? No. You freed me—unintentional, I know, but you still have my gratitude, not my hate." The demon tilted his head to the side, his brow furrowed as he stared at me like he was trying to drill into my mind. "What is going on in that head of yours?"

But his lies weren't working on me one bit. Especially since it was a question he damn well had the answer to, considering the bastard could read my thoughts. This was the number one reason I didn't call his daddy in my head—my self-preservation instincts just a little too acute to sign my own death warrant.

All it would take was one wrong move, and Aemon could have my head. A flash of Agent Bancroft's face filled my brain, her skin graying as blood poured from the slice in her jugular. How hard it was to get the blood out from under my fingernails. The way the earth swallowed her up as Bishop disposed of her body...

The fear I should have felt earlier finally showed up, and I desperately tried to empty my mind as I stared at the demon in my passenger seat. And if I didn't know better, I'd peg the expression on his face as concern.

"When was the last time you slept?" He clucked his

tongue at me much like his father had. "I swear, I heal you all up, and you run yourself ragged in a day?"

"Was I supposed to say thank you for that?" I hissed, a spark of rage making me braver. "Because if I'm not mistaken, you were the reason I needed healing in the first place." The memory of my chest ripping open, of his spirit clawing its way out of me made the burn on my sternum ache, and I fought the urge to touch it again.

"True," he mused, his gaze skating over me like a physical touch, "and I apologize for my rudeness. I was desperate and manipulated the situation to get free. It was bad form."

Snorting, I relaxed away from the door, allowing myself to settle back into my seat. "Bad form? Is that demon-speak for utter and complete bullshit? Because that would be closer to the mark."

My snark seemed to amuse him, his mouth lifting at the corners. "Point made. Though you still haven't answered my question. When was the last time you slept?"

The chuckle that escaped my mouth was dark as I started the Jeep and cranked the air-conditioning. "Well, the last time I got any sleep, *someone* hijacked my body and had me waking up in a cemetery of all places." My shudder was involuntary, the summer heat of the cab doing nothing to combat the memory. "Fun fact: I hate cemeteries. *Hate* them. But I especially hate them at night. I know torture is your game and all, but that was just rude."

Aemon's lips curved as if he were holding in a laugh —the bastard. "My apologies, Miss," he replied, giving me a truncated bow. "But who wouldn't want to spend more time with you? Honestly, I'd take all the time I could get."

Leaning over once more, he rested his chin on his fist as he plucked my phone from the cupholder. "You really do need sleep, though."

As soon as he said the word, my eyelids got heavier, my struggle to hold them up almost more than I could take. "What are you doing?" I asked, reaching for the device. He held it away from me as he powered it down. "Give that back."

In addition to my battle to keep my eyes open, my arms seemed to be made of lead and my legs encased in cement. And despite all that, I still sensed him leaning closer to me. Before I thought better of it, I had a blade out of its sheathe and against his throat, my eyes fighting to stay open.

Hell, I hadn't even told my hand to do it, but the

shiny glint of the knife at his throat made my eyes lose the war.

"What's stopping me from slitting your throat?" I mumbled, struggling to keep the blade against his skin as my lids fluttered closed.

The bastard chuckled. *Chuckled.* As if I were cute or something.

"Probably because you and I both know that blade wouldn't kill me. Hell, it wouldn't even slow me down." His voice took on a soothing quality, and sleep dared to pull me under. "I'm a Prince of Hell, my angry little flower. No knife is going to hurt me."

"Good for you," I slurred, my words floaty as if I'd already dropped off, as the quiet mechanical whir of my seat reclining filtered through the air.

His dark chuckle made me want to press the blade harder against his skin, but I couldn't quite manage it. "Get some rest," he murmured, running a finger down my cheek. "And don't worry. You can try to kill me again when you wake up."

And I would, too.

Probably.


When my eyelids managed to peel themselves open, the full moon was peeking through the broken spires of the burned-out cathedral. It took a minute for me to remember where I was and a little bit longer to remember that I wasn't alone.

I shot to sitting, and the change in position had my head swimming for a second. Aemon didn't pay me any mind. Instead, he flipped the blade I'd once pressed against his neck over and over in the air. With each flip, he caught the weapon either by the tip or the hilt, his fingers moving blindingly fast.

"What the fuck?" I squawked, staring at the demon prince just sitting there as calm as you please. "What did you do to me?"

The side of Aemon's mouth curled up in a little smirk. "Feel better? Rested?"

Raising my seat up, I glared at the man. "That's not the point."

His grin got wider, taking over both sides of his mouth. "Of course it is. You're too proud to take sleep medication—either that or you enjoy being a martyr. You'd been awake about two days and some change by my calculations, and your kind can't go too long without sleep."

"Oh, you know my kind, do you?" What a load of crap. And martyr? What kind of psychoanalyst bullshit was this?

"Of course I do. You're a grave talker and a daughter of Death. You need more food than the average college football player, more sleep than a sloth, and you have an overdeveloped sense of responsibility for shit that is not your fucking problem." Aemon snorted, laughing at his own joke as he tossed the blade again.

My skin nearly blistered with the heat of my rage. Unbidden, my hand shot out, snatching the dagger from the air before it could land back in his hand. "You don't know me."

"Again, of course I do." He tapped his temple. "I spent a fair number of days in your head before Daddy Dearest kicked me out. Granted, it was rather crowded in there, but I got the gist."

Heat flashed over my skin as the embarrassment settled deep in my chest. He'd seen a hell of a lot more than just my psyche. I had to grit my teeth to keep from screaming or punching him or running from the Jeep like my hair was on fire.

Instead, I settled on interrogation.

"What's your angle here? You had plenty of chances to kill me. Why didn't you?"

Aemon sobered as he stared straight out the window, not looking at me for once. I couldn't tell if I enjoyed the reprieve from his piercing blue gaze or if I hated that he was hiding something.

Both, probably.

"No angle," he murmured, steepling his fingers. "You needed rest, and I owed you one."

*Owed me one? Is that what he called it?*

"You took over my body, killed two witches with my hands, and landed your fucking daddy on my doorstep. You owe me more than *one*." We would never be even— not after what he'd taken.

Aemon pursed his lips, nodding. "I know."

Fighting the urge to roll my eyes, I asked, "Why are you here?"

His mouth tipped up on one side. "Who wouldn't want the joy of your company? Personally, I find you completely irresistible."

"Cut the shit, Aemon," I barked, tightening my grip on the knife I'd stolen back. Somehow, it was now pointing in his direction. *Oh, well.* "You want something. Everyone always does. Out with it."

The demon huffed, not looking at me again. "That's just it, isn't it? Everyone always wants something. Always needs you to fight their battles for them or wants to take another thing from you. Even me. I took what was not mine to have."

If I gritted my teeth any harder, they'd be cracked nubs. "And?"

"And it makes me wonder," he began, shifting his

weight so he was now looking me in the eye, "if the people you love—that you assume love you—actually give a shit that you're drowning. Because you are. Drowning, I mean. It makes me wonder what you'd be when you find someone who only wants you for you, and not for what you can give them."

Heat raced all the way up my spine, suffusing my cheeks when it had nowhere else to go. I couldn't tell what was worse: him implying that I was only a convenience for the people around me or that in the deepest, darkest parts of me, I feared he was right.

*Another bit of torture, just like your fucking father.*

"Get out—*out* of my car and out of my *fucking* head." He was wrong. I had J and Jimmy. They didn't always want something from me. And Dave. And Sloane. I had friends. I had a family. I wasn't just a free-for-all of doing shit for people.

He was wrong.

He was.

Aemon's expression turned sad for a second, only a dash coloring his features before it was gone. "As you wish."

*Pity. A demon pities me. Perfect.*

But before I could give him another piece of my mind, he winked out of sight, leaving me alone in the cab once more. Then I realized what I'd done.

"Fuck," I growled, slapping my hand against the steering wheel. "Now I have to find him again."

*Man, Ingrid is going to be pissed.*

## 13

It felt like my life had become one big thing I didn't want to do after another. I stared at my phone and contemplated just how shady *not* telling Ingrid would be. For fuck's sake, I'd just lost the demon we'd been looking for because my *"feelings"* got hurt. Considering the thought made me want to vomit, I figured pretty fucking shady.

*Fine.*

Pressing the "Call" button, I prayed she continued her trend of not picking up. Then I could leave an awkward voicemail instead of admitting I'd let Aemon slip through my fingers. And usually, I'd rather throw my whole phone in a running blender than leave a voicemail. That hell was preferable to this.

As soon as she answered—because of course she did

precisely when I didn't want her to—I blurted out a hurried, "I fucked up."

Silence rattled down the line for about three beats too long before she replied, "I'm sorry, this is Darby Adler, right?"

"Yes, you impudent little shit."

Ingrid snickered. "There she is. Okay, Miss Perfect. How did you fuck up?"

"Aemon was in my car when I left the nest," I began, but I didn't get out the rest before she interrupted me.

"I swear to the Fates above, you need a keeper. Where was your backup—you know the boyfriend I can't stand? Where was his stupid ass when a demon just showed up in your car?"

Pinching my brow, I sighed. "Not there. I may have told him I didn't want to see him for a while. But that's not the poi—"

Ingrid whooped down the line. "Halle-fucking-lujah. About time you got rid of his weaselly ass. Okay, so Aemon was in your car. Considering you're still breathing, I take it the interaction wasn't violent?"

Thumping my head on my steering wheel, I struggled to explain just how nonviolent the conversation had been. "No, not violent. Um, it was weird, actually. He... made me take a nap."

"I'm confused. Is 'taking a nap' code for something?"

"No, it's not code for anything. He said I'd been awake too long and I needed sleep, and then he just, well, made me sleep." Then I blurted the rest. "He apologized for possessing me, and then he told me that I was making myself a martyr, and I worry about shit that's not my problem. He said people don't see I'm drowning, and then I got mad and told him to get out of my car."

By the time I got all of it out, I was breathing hard, but Ingrid was laughing her head off. "Oh, my god, that is fucking adorable. This would only happen to you. I have to tell Mags this shit. She's going to roll on the floor—especially after I tell her you're kicking La Roux to the curb."

"I didn't say I was kicking Bishop to the curb," I protested weakly. Okay, so Bishop and I had major problems that I didn't think we could fix, but I couldn't just end it. Not after everything we'd been through.

Right?

*You don't even have his phone number, you dumb bitch. You've never been to his house. He's pulled a one-eighty going Mach twelve after saying the big "L" like a minute ago. You've dropped men a lot quicker for way less. Get it together.*

If only my inner bitch was this on point with the hard truths all the time.

"Back to the reason I called, you turd. I let Aemon

get away. He was so close, and now Deimos is going to use you as bait or something to lure in your stupid sire and trap his son. I fucked up, Ingrid."

Her chuckles tapered off, but the mirth never left her voice. "You didn't do anything of the sort. You were trapped in a car with a Prince of Hell. I know you're a badass and everything, but what were you supposed to do? Tackle him? Yell for his father and have Aemon kill you?"

She brought up a good point, but I couldn't even agree with her because she was on a roll.

"And using me as bait is logical and necessary. If Deimos and Aemon want Nero dead, I'm all for it. So what you let him get away. We'll have another opportunity."

Groaning, I picked my head up and stared at the house. "You're letting me off easy."

"So what if I am? It's my maker and my trauma, so that means I get to do what I want."

How was I going to argue with that? "Fine. Be awesome, why don't you."

"I will. Now go inside before your best friend throws another fit. Cooper really does love leaving voicemails." With that, the little jerk hung up on me, and I was left with nothing to do but go inside.

Since the universe had decided not to grant me any

favors, those twelve hours I'd been asleep did not go unnoticed. As soon as I turned my phone on to call Ingrid, a veritable cornucopia of texts and voicemails bombarded my inbox. Most were from J, but Jimmy, Tobin, and even Dave had left a few. Still, one person was conspicuously absent from my notifications.

Detaching my ass from my seat, I trudged into the house, the lethargy I'd started with gone but not forgotten. As soon as I opened the door, the yelling started.

"Where have you been?" J half-shouted, his hands on his hips like he was my mother. "I have called every single person I could think of to locate your ass. Hell, even Tobin tried, but your phone was off. With a demon on the loose, why would you turn your phone off?"

Dutifully, I ignored my best friend and waved at his boyfriend who was lounging on the couch, seemingly without a care in the world. "Hi, Jimmy."

His eyes twinkled as he rose to corral J. "I told you she'd be fine," he murmured in J's ear as he wrapped an arm around his shoulder. "My protection charm is working perfectly. Plus, we asked Sloane, and what did she say?"

J rolled his eyes. "That she wasn't dead and to tell her she said 'hi' when we saw her again." My best friend glared at me. "So, your sister says 'hi,' by the way. Wanna tell me where you were?"

I did not want a repeat of my confession to Ingrid. "Taking an involuntary nap."

J sobered. "Oh, shit. Did you not sleep after I dropped you off?"

"That, I did not."

He went to hug me but stopped short. "What do you mean by 'involuntary'? Care to explain that bit?"

"Absolutely not," I muttered, completing the embrace where he left off. There was no way I wanted to start that conversation. Nuh-uh. No way, no how.

J squeezed me tighter, a chuckle getting the better of him. "I'll get it out of you somehow, D. I always do."

Unfortunately, unless the jerk wanted to keep his head in the sand, I pretty much told him everything. I hated it when he was right.

In the middle of our hug, the front door opened behind me.

"What are you doing here?" J barked, using the cop voice he so rarely employed.

Turning, I got a good look as to why. Bishop now stood in the Warden house living room as if he had the right to walk in without so much as a knock. Windblown and harried, La Roux seemed more than a little out of sorts. "Looking for Darby, same as you were an hour ago when I got the call she was missing. Have a habit of losing your partner, Cooper?"

I knew damn well that J would do no such thing. He wouldn't call Bishop unless I was dying, and even then, he'd probably cut off a toe first.

"Darby can take care of herself," J replied, his tone amiable, even though his jaw was tighter than a drum. "What I want to know is why you're walking into this house like you own it."

That was an answer I wanted, too, but I wasn't going to air out my relationship drama in the living room—especially since I caught a glimpse of Tobin and Acker peeking out of the kitchen to stare at us.

"Down, Killer. I got it." Giving J's stomach a gentle punch, I gestured for Bishop to walk right back out the door he'd just entered. "Let's go have a talk."

This brought up memories of the first time I tried ejecting Bishop from my house. It hadn't worked that time, but my hope was that this one would be more successful. A flash of hurt crossed his eyes for a moment before he ducked his head and strode out the front door. I was half-tempted to just close it behind him and lock it, the sting of his words last night still weighing on me. But like the totally adult woman I was, I followed him to the front porch and shut the door behind me.

I was under no illusion that J and Jimmy—and

probably Tobin and Acker—weren't listening on the other side. Hell, if Yazzie was somewhere in the house, he could hear me no matter how low I pitched my voice.

Pretend. I could still pretend no one else would hear this bullshit.

Bishop sauntered over to the railing, gripping it as if he'd like to rip it from its fastenings, but his face remained neutral.

"So, you're still mad at me, huh?" he muttered, his tone seemingly baffled, even though I could not have been any clearer last night. "I was tired, too, you know."

This was *not* a good start. Hell, this wasn't even in the same direction as a good start.

"Since you have yet to change your attitude or apologize? Yeah. I'm still mad. And I'm not going to dignify that 'tired' shit with a response. Take responsibility for your fucking actions or get off my porch." Not that taking responsibility for that shit would do him any good now.

"I just don't get it," he growled, throwing his hands up. "Day before yesterday, we were fine. Then that damn demon came along, and you're acting differently."

But I wasn't. I was acting the same as I always did. It was him that was acting differently. It was him who had gone from sweet and kind to an absolute fucking douchebag. "No, two days ago, you acted normal, and yesterday you turned into a complete flaming asshole. Being rude to the guard, talking to me like I'm a piece of shit. But it's more than that."

Bishop shifted away from the railing, his arms open wide. "Enlighten me then."

"I don't know you." The truth of that hit me somewhere underneath my ribs, the sting sharp.

Bishop scoffed, staring at me like I was crazy. "Yes, you do. You know everything there is to know about me."

"No," I insisted. "I don't. I've never called you. Not once. You know why?" I waited for him to answer me, but he couldn't. "Because I don't have your number. You've never given me basic contact information, other than a fake FBI card that reroutes me to the ABI. I started thinking about it, and I've never had to call you. You always just show up."

"And saved your ass, but what of it?" he asked, his tone more than a little dismissive. "I'll give you my number right no—"

"Not the point, Bishop." Jesus, I was going to have to spell it out for him, wasn't I? "The point is, I've never had it. You know what else I don't know? Where you live. I've never been to your home. You've never even mentioned it. Not once. I don't know who your friends are. Sarina, sure, but who else? In five hundred years, is she your only friend? Your family—which is a sore subject, I get it—but I don't know their names. And even though they gave you up, someone had to take care of you. So, who raised you? Who kissed your boo-boos as a kid? Where do you call home?"

My rapid-fire questions seemed to make him uncomfortable, but all this needed to be said.

"I don't know you. You know everything about me—courtesy of tidbits from Sarina and me just fucking telling you—but I don't know *you*. And it isn't from a lack of me asking, either. You've been party to some of the worst, most significant parts of my life, and I don't know that first fucking thing about yours."

"So, this is it?" he growled, moving into my space, towering over me like a threat. "I don't tell you my life story, and you toss me to the curb like I'm trash?" Eyes flashing, teeth bared, this wasn't a man that was sorry for hurting me or trying to hold onto what we had.

This was different.

Just like with Aemon, my blade found its way under his chin before I ever told it to move. With Aemon, I hadn't needed to use it, but with Bishop? I feared I most definitely would.

"Back up," I warned, not even blinking. "Now."

Bishop's gold eyes flared as his power rose on the air, the pressure of it skating over my skin but not landing.

*Was he…? No. Huh-uh.*

There was no way he was trying to use that power against me. No way he could manipulate me like that. But he didn't move—he didn't budge so much as an inch.

"The woman you claim to love puts a knife to your throat because she believes you'll hurt her, and what do you do?"

That got his attention.

Bishop took a step back, his eyes and power not ramping down an inch. My stomach pitched as nausea crawled up my throat. This wasn't right—right? There was no way I could have been this blind. I'd seen so many domestics in my line of work—both as a beat cop and as a detective.

How did I not see him for what he was?

And the awful part? He didn't seem to care that he was proving all my points just by acting this way.

"It's time for you to leave, boy," a deadly yet silky-smooth voice called from the lawn. Deimos' once-mismatched gaze blazed red as it locked on Bishop. "Before she has to make you."

I most definitely did not want to make him, but I would if I had to.

As the door opened, the ratchet of a shotgun chambering a round rang out. I didn't even spare my best friend a glance. I knew damn well my backup had arrived.

"Like the man said," Jimmy hissed, appearing behind Bishop, sword in hand, "it's time for you to leave."

A dark chuckle reached my ears. "Is it wrong that I hope he doesn't take the hint?" Yazzie remarked from the yard behind Deimos. "I'd love to see her kick your ass."

Next to Yazzie were Tobin and Acker—the former seeming uncomfortable with the confrontation, and the latter slapping a baseball bat against his open palm.

*Shotguns and baseball bats on the front fucking lawn. Welcome to Tennessee, folks.*

"This," I said, gesturing with the knife between us, "is done. You and me? *We're* done. Don't come back here. Understand?"

Bishop's power died as he took a giant step back, his irises bleeding back to dark brown as the swirls of magic circling his arms faded. What I could only assume was shock flitted over his expression as his chin lifted, but it was there and gone in a flash.

"We're not done, Adler. You and me? We'll never be done." And then the man himself vanished, melting into the night once more without so much as a word.

Saliva pooled in my mouth as nausea ramped up once again. The disbelief and that damn ache were both back in full force, causing what was left of my shriveled heart to shudder just a bit. I wanted to say thanks for the backup, wanted to tell them just how much it meant for all of them to show up for me—either that or go curl up in a dark corner and cry my fucking eyes out.

Instead, I asked, "Which one of you called him? Because whoever did now owes me food."

My gaze laser-locked on Yazzie's pitiful flinch, coupled with his raised hand. "It was me, but" —He raised the other hand in surrender—"you two were together like a day ago. I thought he'd want to know his woman was missing."

I tried to keep my eye from twitching, the adrenaline of ending it with Bishop making that feat damn near impossible. By the way all three agents took a step back, I was unsuccessful. Sucking in a calming breath, I sheathed the blade I'd pressed to Bishop's throat.

"Fine. I forgive you. You still owe me food, though. And *not* tacos. I want barbecue. And a lot of it."

If I ate another taco again, it might be too soon—a thought that pissed me off more than I could say. The man had ruined tacos for me.

*What kind of a bastard ruins tacos?*

Yazzie snickered, fishing his keys from his pocket. "On it, boss."

"Thanks," I whispered, refusing to let my emotions get the better of me. "To all of you. Thanks for showing up."

Yazzie dipped his head before rotating on a heel, and Acker and Tobin followed him as he raced for the detached garage. Good. I hoped J informed them of just how much I could eat because I was starving.

A question bloomed in my mind, and I whipped my gaze to Deimos. "He wasn't possessed, right? Bishop, I mean. You'd know, wouldn't you?"

Deimos' smile was positively smug. "Yes, I'd know. And no, your former boyfriend is not possessed by any demon, Fae, or spirit that I can see."

"He's not spelled, either," Jimmy answered my next question before I could ask it. "No, his problem is that he's just an asshole."

"Maybe he got hit too hard when Aemon dumped him on his ass," J muttered as he cleared the shotgun. "Maybe he's having a psychotic break. Who knows?"

If I hadn't have healed him all up from Aemon's assault, maybe that TBI thing would have had merit, but his behavior just didn't make any sense. But it wasn't like I could cry about it right then or eat my weight in ice cream. I had a god on my doorstep for the second time this week. This bullshit called for a drink.

"Please tell me there is some kind of alcohol in this place," I pleaded, rubbing the crease between my brows. I didn't wait for an answer, instead choosing to find the booze myself. Pivoting on a heel, I walked right back inside the house to rummage in the kitchen for the good stuff.

This level of drama required hard liquor, good barbecue, and a distraction. Since Deimos was here, I had one of those covered.

"While I appreciate the assist," I said, opening the upper cabinets in my search for libations, "you typically want something. Out with it, please. I have booze to drink, barbecue to eat, and if I'm lucky, I'll get another good nap in the next day or two."

And maybe somewhere in there, I'd process what had just happened with Bishop.

*He used his magic on you—or tried to. What's left to process?*

Blinking back angry tears, I continued my search for whatever booze I could get my hands on. It didn't need to be vodka. Tequila would do. Even gin or whiskey. Hell, I'd take peach schnapps or cooking wine at this point. And if I found chocolate in the process, well, then all the better.

The god's chuckle was made of nightmares, but I'd take mirth over male rage right now. "It's time for your small friend to contact her maker. I figured you'd want to be there for her since it will be trying."

I stopped my search to stare at the god, his mismatched eyes the picture of innocence.

"Bullshit. You've been nothing but antagonistic since I met you. Granted, the help was welcomed—I'll give you that—but kindness? Try again and be honest this time."

"Can't I turn over a new leaf?" At my continued stare, he rolled his eyes. "Fine. Your sister said that if I continued unnecessarily tormenting you, she'd tattle on me to Persephone. Have you ever seen that woman mad? No, thank you. There are things even I fear, child."

Snorting, I continued my search. "That, I will believe."

"Your sister is formidable, I will give you that, but tattling is just rude. She's nothing like your father. Azrael would have just raised an eyebrow at me and muttered something about Fate or some other such nonsense."

"That sounds like Azrael. *Ah ha*," I crowed, my fingers closing around my prize. In the very back of the freezer was a frosty bottle of top-shelf vodka. "You knew my father, right? But you weren't friends. More like work associates, I'm guessing."

Taking the glass offered by J, I poured myself a healthy measure and slugged it back. The alcohol burned as it went down, going a long way to taking the edge off the bullshit we'd just gone through.

"In a manner of speaking. We were cordial enough, but Azrael wasn't big on punishment. Not his fault. Most people can't stomach what I do." Deimos conjured his own cup, sipping the mystery beverage. "Your sister, though? That woman was made of vengeance. She has no problem delivering souls to me."

"And that's a compliment in your world?" J asked, pouring me another drink. He seemed completely fine with the God of Torment just chilling in this kitchen, which made me think he didn't know who Deimos was.

"It is. Vengeance and justice are paramount in Tartarus. Without them, I would not have a purpose. And speaking of justice," Deimos began before taking a gulp of his drink, "I am owed a soul and wish to collect."

More like Aemon was owed a soul, and Deimos was owed Aemon, but whatever.

Tossing back my new drink, I contemplated just how odd my life was. There was my human best friend, his Fae boyfriend, and a literal god in my kitchen. Well, not mine, but close enough. There was probably a joke in there somewhere, but I wasn't drunk enough to find it.

"And just how are we going to contact Nero? I doubt his number is listed in the yellow pages." I turned to J. "Do people even use phone books anymore, or am I dating myself?"

"Dating yourself," J replied, pulling a bottle of gin from the fridge. "I haven't seen a phone book in ten years."

Shrugging, I sipped my vodka, the warmth of the alcohol finally hitting my limbs. "Still. I don't know how to contact him. Do you?"

"Your friend Ingrid will help with that."

Vague, but okay. "I don't see her anywhere. Are we going to her or...?"

Deimos' smile was patronizing, but being three shots of vodka in, I really didn't care. "All vampires can call their sire through the blood bond. Those as old as Ingrid can send a message or summon them at will. I expect your friend any time now to perform the ritual. She doesn't want to summon him anywhere near her nest, but she needs a highly warded property situated on a solid ley line. She'll be here shortly."

The doorbell rang not a moment later, proving Deimos right.

"I'll get it," Jimmy announced, walking back to the front door.

A moment later, J, Deimos, and I followed him to the living room or parlor or whatever the fuck people called the front room of a house like this. Ingrid's tiny frame was followed by a behemoth bald man with a familiar face. Björn scanned the room for threats before his gaze landed on me.

I'd been under the impression that Björn was a warlock of some kind with the wand-waving and everything, but if he was guarding Ingrid, then maybe not.

"Good to see you again, Warden," Björn greeted with a deferential nod, his gaze never staying in one spot. He was protecting her...

My laugh was part shock and part amazement. "The enforcer of the Dubois nest has a bodyguard? You know it's rude to give me that without also giving me someone to giggle about it with."

Ingrid's smile was mostly feral as she, too, kept her head on a swivel. "Go giggle about it with your boyfriend then."

That blow landed a little harder than she'd intended, making me suck in a breath. "Ow. Well, since I no longer have one of those, I guess I'll just have to giggle by myself."

Her feral smile morphed into a stone-faced frown so quick it would have been comical if her remark didn't still smart. "I talked to you less than half an hour ago. What the fuck happened in thirty minutes that made you go from wishy-washy to broken up?" She cracked her knuckles and her neck, her grin coming back—more genuine this time now that she had a potential opponent to smash. "Also—unrelated—can I throw you a party?"

"Bishop happened," J answered for me while I swiveled on a heel to forage for more vodka and maybe some food.

*A loaf of bread would be nice. Or maybe my weight in gelato. Yeah.*

"He did *what?*" Ingrid shrieked, her small voice ringing like a gong in my head.

Okay, so maybe I wouldn't have that fourth shot. Carefully, I set down my glass as I gritted my teeth. I would not cry—not over that man. Not right now, anyway. Bishop had tried to use his magic on me. I'd felt it skate over my skin and not land—either Jimmy's necklace or Aemon's touch or Azrael's gift protecting me. It didn't matter *why* it didn't land—not really. It mattered that he'd cast it at all.

Why would he do that?

Was he just that desperate not to lose me?

Or was it something else?

I had a sinking feeling in my gut that it was the latter, and in the middle of the unrest here, his actions didn't fill me with warm and fuzzies. Not in the slightest.

This thought burned a hole in my gut as I foraged for food in the fridge, only coming up with a handful of cheddar slices and a package of hard salami. Give me a bundle of grapes, and I was a hop, skip, and a jump from a charcuterie board.

Absently, I munched on the cheese and meat while sipping my vodka. So what if I broke up with my boyfriend. There were more important things to do.

*Then finish your pity party and get your shit together. Ingrid needs you.*

Stuffing the last slice of cheese and cold cuts in my mouth, I managed to get my shit together enough to walk back into the parlor. Ingrid's face was a mottled purple, her eyes vamped out and her fangs descended in full force. It made me wonder just what J had seen or what Deimos had told her.

"You held a dagger to his throat?" she hissed as soon as she locked eyes with me. "What—*exactly*—made you think you needed to do that, Darby?"

*To tell her or to not tell her.* The best I could do was shrug.

"That's not an answer," she griped, fitting her tiny fists on her hips.

Tossing my hands up, I abandoned the group to sit on the couch. "It's the only one you're going to get. Don't we have better things to do than talk about my former relationship? Like contacting Nero or solving world hunger or discussing cold fusion?"

At this point, I'd rather do evidence chain of custody forms than this.

"Are we doing this?"

Grumbling, Ingrid moved through the house, heading for the backyard, all of us following her like she was our mama duck. I'd only been out here once, and I'd been so focused on Sloane and Linus that I hadn't taken in the manicured space.

The covered porch wrapped around the house and led down to a courtyard filled with flowers and ornamental trees, the late spring air carrying the warm scent of blooms through the air. The brick pathway curved into a circle, bisected by crisscrossing trails, a bubbling fountain depicting a woman pouring from a pitcher at the center. To the naked eye, it was a standard courtyard. From here, it almost appeared as if the intersecting paths were a star—a pentagram, maybe?

"Who owned this house before us?" I asked, a wariness to my steps as I made my way down the porch stairs. Someone already tried spelling me once today. The last thing I needed was getting blown off my feet because I was dumb enough to cross a witch's circle.

Ingrid traversed the circular path first, easing my fears quite a bit. "The Knoxville coven, but that was nearly a century ago. They had to surrender it to the ABI to pay for sanctions or something, and the ABI gave it to the council for the same reason."

"That explains the ley lines." Witches were famous for building their coven houses over ley lines to draw in power. It's why the Knoxville coven had built Whisper Lake to try and keep Azrael down. They needed that concentrated well of power to draw from. "Okay, so how do you do this—call him, I mean?"

Ingrid hugged her elbows, her shoulders hunched in a way that made her resemble the child she was when turned. "I have to spill blood. But luckily I'm safe here."

That didn't make me feel warm and fuzzy.

"Why do you need to be safe?" J asked—a pertinent question in my opinion. "No offense to you, but why summon him here? Won't that put everyone in the house in danger? Isn't this guy some kind of ancient murder vamp?"

Ingrid rolled her eyes, a bit of the fear bleeding from her expression. "No, dummy. We're doing it here because of the protection this ground offers. He can't come here, and he won't know where I summoned him from, just the city."

I couldn't say that made me feel any better, but it was a start.

Rolling her shoulders, she stared at the sky as she gathered herself. There was no reality where my small friend could be this afraid. If there was ever a question of how bad Nero actually was, Ingrid's fear told me far more than I needed to know.

Sucking in a huge breath, Ingrid's eyes never left the sky as she held her hand out to Björn. Dutifully, he slapped a small knife in her palm, but he didn't seem happy about it.

"Stop." I heard myself say, my brain catching up just a touch too late. "She doesn't have to do this. I can look for him. I can—"

Deimos held up a hand. "This is the fastest way to get what we need. It's awful, yes. Painful. But when Nero meets his end, Ingrid will know she had a hand in it. Your friend will have vengeance. And that is better than avoiding the pain now. He slid his gaze to Ingrid, who was giving him a beatific smile. "Right?"

"I like the way you think," she murmured before sucking in another breath. Before she let it out again, she sliced the blade from her wrist to elbow.

Blood poured from her flesh, dripping to the brick

pavers at the center of the pentagram. She thrashed her arm, flinging the droplets over the flowers and the fountain before raising both hands to the sky as she threw her head back. Her red eyes rolled back in her head as she let out an unholy bellow, the scream coming from her mouth chilling me to the bone.

Magic flowed from Ingrid—not like Bishop's and not like mine. No, this was primal, crude, and altogether different, but magic, nonetheless.

"Jesus fucking Christ," J muttered, eyes wide as he stared at my small friend, his hand gripping mine.

*My sentiments exactly.*

I shot a bewildered look at Deimos, but he didn't meet my gaze, a frown etching into his forehead as he surveyed Ingrid's call.

Quickly, her scream tapered off, her bloody arms— now all healed up—lowering as she worried her lip. She shook her head, her brow furrowed.

"It didn't work," she muttered, her puzzled expression meeting mine. "He—he's not there. I called and it's as if he wasn't listening." She shifted her gaze to Deimos. "I'm sorry. I tried, but I don't think he's going to answer me."

But I knew that none of us were ever that lucky. Ingrid feared her call didn't work?

Well, I feared that it did.

## 15

After Ingrid's failed—according to her—call to her sire, the boys came back with enough barbecue to clean out an entire restaurant. Granted, this would only last me about a day—especially with all the people in this house—but I commended them on securing food at this hour.

Ingrid, Björn, and Deimos stayed for a bit, but each left once they realized I didn't talk much while I was eating. Before she left, Ingrid put a hand on my arm.

"Do me a favor, okay?" she asked in the middle of my second rack of ribs, earning herself a grunt in response. "Please—for me—don't ever turn into a vampire or a ghoul. You'd never make it out of your first year with an appetite like this."

Yes, I had sauce all over my face and hands. Yes, I ate

like *Cookie Monster*. But I was hungry, dammit. Hell, J and I had a rule where he pretended I wasn't there so he didn't ask me questions and annoy me. Because getting in between me and food was dangerous.

I flipped her off with my sauced middle finger, while still chowing down on my ribs.

"I love you, too," she muttered, showing herself out, with Björn in her wake.

Yazzie let out a dark chuckle. "Also, maybe don't get bit by a lycanthrope? You'd be a complete menace."

Lycanthropes were bitten and diseased humans, infected with a specific type of rabies that mutated their DNA. Then they turned into grotesque half-man, half-animal creatures on the full moon. I'd never come across them before, but I'd heard about a whole pack of them that'd been taken out in a week up in Ascension. I didn't know who'd done the honors, but I was glad it hadn't been me.

"I'll put it on my list," I grumbled around a bone, stripping the last of the meat from it. "There's more burnt ends, right?"

By the time I was moderately satiated, nearly everyone—including J and Jimmy—had gone upstairs to bed. Acker had found them a room, and I couldn't begin to say just how awesome it was to have my partner in this house and sleeping under my roof. It felt safer somehow, even though I knew having him here put him in more danger.

I'd have to make sure Jimmy made him a necklace like mine. And maybe a bubble. A case could definitely be made for the bubble.

Almost full, I'd officially stalled long enough. After I'd attacked my hands with a wet wipe—*or four*—I picked up my phone and dialed one of my least favorite people in the world. Snorting, the humor of it hit me. I had the number for Thomas Gao—ancient vampire, former vampire king of Knoxville, and co-leader of the Night Watch—and I still didn't have Bishop's.

All it took was three rings to get his overly snooty voice to rattle down the line. "What do you want?"

Rolling my eyes—even though I knew he couldn't see—I patiently waited for a more cordial greeting.

"Fine. Hello, Warden Adler. How may I be of service?"

That wasn't much better, but I'd take it. "It's about our mutual friend."

"We have several. To which mutual friend are you referring?"

It was true. Thomas was half in love with my sister, even though she was taken by a hunky elemental mage. Our friend group was vast and varied. But I wouldn't be calling him about any of those people. I would call him about the vampire he thought of like a daughter.

"Ingrid, you dope," I groused. "Why would I call you about anyone else? In fact, I would have called you sooner—as soon as I knew—but I was indisposed."

"Elaborate. Now," Thomas growled, the ancient vampire adding a little of his magic into his voice.

"Quit it. You know that doesn't work on us. If I didn't want to tell you, I would have just not called, you moron. Now, this is a doozy, so buckle up and don't interrupt me," I ordered, irritated he'd try that vampire voice mojo bullshit. Still, Ingrid was his family, and if I were in the middle of the same bout of bullshit, she'd call my family, too.

By the time I was finished with the Aemon-Nero-Deimos drama, Thomas was seething. "And you couldn't have called me sooner?"

Dropping my fork in the remnants of my baked beans, I pitched my voice low so I wouldn't wake the whole fucking house. "No, I was taking an involuntary nap, then broke up with my boyfriend, and by that time, Deimos was already here wanting to call Nero. I couldn't exactly fit in a courtesy call."

Thomas snorted, the indelicate sound so odd coming from him. "What the hell do you mean by 'involuntary nap'?"

"A demon made me go night-night, Thomas. What part of the word 'involuntary' is unclear to you?"

The roar of laughter I got had me pulling the phone from my ear so he wouldn't shatter my eardrum. "It's not funny."

"Yes, it is. It's perfect," he said, still chuckling. "Fine. You called as soon as you could, and I appreciate the heads-up."

"Super. Glad you're onboard. Could you please keep your ear to the ground? Ingrid doesn't think the blood bond call worked, but—"

"You do." His sigh was exhausted enough that I could only nod. I knew that level of tired. "If there's a vampire I don't want in town, it's that man, but if it gets him out of the picture, I can't be mad at it. I'll keep her safe, Darby." And then the dick hung up without so much as a farewell.

*Jerk.*

Now that *that* mess was over, I stowed my meager leftovers and headed upstairs for bed. Sure, I'd gotten a twelve-hour nap, but my sleep deficit was still in the red. My quest for sleep was derailed as soon as I saw the stack of files on the foot of my bed.

Tobin had said he'd have a preliminary report for me by the end of the day, but the foot-tall mountain of files was not what I was expecting. Hefting the pile, I moved them to the nightstand and attempted to ignore the fount of knowledge all but begging to be read.

Sleep, dammit. I needed more of it and obsessing over a case to not feel my emotions wasn't going to help. Instead, I changed into pajamas—my butter-soft lounge pants and a baggy Nirvana concert T-Shirt that I'd stolen fair and square from my dad. It still hurt that his scent wasn't on it anymore—too many washings over the years robbing it of that precious smell.

Swallowing hard, I plucked a note from my jeans pocket. It was the same note that Sloane had delivered from the Underworld—the one my dad had written to me. I hadn't gathered the courage yet to read it, and as I turned it over and over in my hands, I wondered if I ever could. Stuffing that bit of ache down, I gently slipped the folded paper into the pocket of my pajamas.

I managed to wash my face—not crying and not thinking—before the call of the files on my nightstand grew far too great. With a toothbrush hanging out of my mouth, I stared at the mountain of information just begging for me to dive in. If Ingrid's call to Nero had actually gone through—and I believed it did—then I needed to know everything about this man.

After spitting out the toothpaste and rinsing my mouth, I scooped up the stack of files and padded downstairs. Snagging a cup of coffee first, I settled in on the floor of the parlor, spreading out the files on the coffee table as I sipped the yummy brew. The thick note in my pocket dug into my skin through the fabric of my pajamas and I fished it out, setting it carefully beside the files. I should have kept it upstairs in a safe spot, but the thought of leaving it anywhere made me ill.

The top file laid out Nero's origins—or what little there was to know about them. Born around 140 BCE, he was the son of a fisherman who joined the Roman army as soon as he possibly could. He moved up the ranks slowly, until one day, a lowly soldier was advanced to *Primus Pilus* only after five years of service in 118 BCE.

Since that note was underlined three times, I searched what the hell a *Primus Pilus* was on my phone only to learn that the title was a commanding officer of the elite troops.

*I'll take the year he made a deal with a Prince of Hell for 500, Alex.*

After that, the records went from standard origin story to fucking horror show of murdered civilians, war-torn conquering, and enough straight pillaging to make me ill. And that had happened before he was turned.

Maker unknown, Nero's bloodlust only ramped up once he'd been made into a vampire.

"See why I want to put him down?" a familiar voice asked, which had me nearly jumping to my feet.

I shot a glare over my shoulder at the demon responsible for all this carnage. Aemon sat calm as you please on the couch behind me, arms splayed wide across the back, seemingly without a care in the world.

"What the fuck are you doing in my house?" I hissed. I should have screamed. Should have yelled the whole damn place down, but I didn't. "How did you get in here? Demons have to be invited in. Or is that just another rule you break?"

Aemon's smug grin widened, flashing a hint of fang. "Those are lower-level incorporeal demons. I am a Prince of Hell. It took two gods to put me in that box, Darby. Do you honestly believe I can be stopped by a ward and a door?"

Of course he didn't need to be invited in. *Just destroy all illusions of safety, why don't you?*

And still, I didn't yell the house down. "Did you do this to me? Make it so I don't scream my head off when you're near? Was that a built-in feature of the brand you put on me?"

Aemon's head rocked back like I'd struck him. "I didn't brand you," he murmured, sitting forward on the couch, leaning close so his face was mere inches from mine. His searing blue eyes pinned me to the spot, and I couldn't move if I wanted to. "Healed you? Yes. Prevented any other of my kind from possessing you?

Also, yes. But branding? That's just rude. I would never."

His breath ghosted across my skin, his voice pitching even lower. "There are many things I would do to that luscious body of yours, my angry little flower, but branding is not one of them."

That didn't explain the burning ache in my chest every time I thought about his healing. It didn't tell me why he was being nice to me when he should want me dead for what my father had done to him. "Then why am I not trying to shoot you in the face right now? Explain that shit to me."

"Maybe you know it won't do any good," he mused, his smile back in full force. "Or maybe you just know I'm not actually a bad guy. I made a bad deal, yes, but I'm not the one who killed those people. I'm not the one who carved a bloody trail through Europe. Nero did that. Had I not been shoved into a tiny box for two millennia, he would have been stopped ages ago."

Sure he would have. Or they would have gone partying together. "And using my body to kill witches makes you a saint? You put blood on my hands, Aemon."

The memory of Bancroft's blood pulsing over my skin, of it crusted under my nails, of it suffusing the lock of that damned coffin filled my brain—I had to fight off the urge to shudder.

Aemon threw his head back, resting it against the top of the couch. "If I recall, those witches were trying to kill you, and by extension, me. I can't feel bad about that, especially since I knew exactly where their souls were going."

He picked his head up, pinning me to the floor with his searing gaze. "Tell me—do you feel that same guilt for killing Mariana? Don't answer that, because I know you don't. You probably wish you'd killed her sooner. Apply that level of apathy to those agents. Trust me. They didn't give that first fuck about killing you. Why feel guilty for beating them to the punch?"

You know it had been a rough day when you started agreeing with a Prince of Hell.

"Why are you here?"

Aemon's gaze left me and landed on the files. "Nice change of subject. Deflection is your forte."

He must have felt my glare because he gave me a shrug. "Just checking in. Making sure you're being taken care of. And a little reconnaissance. You have information I need if I am to collect what I am owed." His head rolled on his neck as his expression turned flirty. "Though, if you don't want to give it to me, I can just stick around. I don't mind the view at all."

Was a single look from a man supposed to leave a girl this scandalized? Or was it just me?

Narrowing my eyes, I decided to hit him where it hurt. "You know, for a demon, you seem a little passive."

His form flickered, along with all the lights in the room, and instead of the blond too-handsome jerk—who seemed to pop up everywhere—was a dense mass of smoke in the vague shape of a man. He tilted his head, his smile going wide as he showed me his impossibly long fangs, his fire eyes blazing in their sockets, the flames trailing up his forehead and into a set of horns.

He was made of torment and screams and darkness, and he scared me more than I thought possible.

Aemon's form flickered back as the lights in the room righted. His suit jacket pristine, his tie perfectly knotted, he brushed an errant lock of hair back from his chiseled cheek.

"You can call it passive, or you can call it polite. I don't have to be an asshole to you. I can just ask you for what I need. Forcing people is not typically my style."

If I didn't sack up, I was going to pee my pants.

Bravado.

I would just have to go the bravado route *because holy fucking shit—what was that?*

"Just me, then?" I quipped, and my voice didn't wobble a bit. Nope. Not at all.

A faint trace of pain pinched his features. "Desperate times," he murmured, the remorse in that tiny sentence hitting me right in the chest. "People do a lot of things they don't want to do when they're backed into a corner. They betray people they'd rather not. They hurt people they care about. They do monstrous things. It's not an excuse, but it is reality."

I thought of all the things I'd done out of desperation —of the people I'd hurt because there was just no other option. Rather than give him a pass, I sipped my cooling coffee.

"Plus," he added, "I did apologize. As you recall, I also made it so it could never happen again while healing you all up. I could have killed your friend and grandfather, but I didn't—especially after your boyfriend's treachery."

Calling Bishop my boyfriend irritated the shit out of me but saying so wouldn't do either of us any good. "Hildy's already dead."

He sat forward on the couch again, and once *again*, he was far too close for my comfort. His gaze glided over my face, taking in whatever expression I had there. "You know what I mean. I could have caused you and yours harm, and I didn't."

A part of me hated that he was right. While we were down, Aemon could have killed us all. He didn't have to leave us to heal on our own. Every single one of us had been unable to fight him. We would have been easy pickings. Another part worried that he was the only reason I'd survived the wolf den—if the power I'd used was mine at all.

It irritated the shit out of me that he'd essentially saved my ass. Twice.

"Fine," I muttered, climbing to my feet. I couldn't stay in this room—not with him. Not now. "Why don't you read up on what one of your deals has wrought? That's why you came here, right? For information?" I pointed at the stack of files. "Well, there it is. I thought I knew monsters, but this..." I couldn't continue that sentence. Nero's blood-soaked history had made my food almost come up more than once.

Pivoting on a heel, I started to leave, when a warm hand caught my wrist.

"Don't forget this," Aemon murmured, gently rotating my wrist and placing my father's note onto the open palm of the hand he held hostage. "It seems important."

Instinctively, my fingers closed around the paper, clutching it tightly as I waited for Aemon to let me go. Then his touch was gone, and I rushed from the parlor, not really knowing where I was going until I found myself in the center of the courtyard.

With the cool bricks of the pathway under my feet, I watched the sky change from dark as pitch, to purple to pink, and finally to orange as the sun peeked over the horizon.

And it didn't matter how much I wanted to know what my father had said, I still couldn't bring myself to read the note in my hand.

## 16

A flash of gray nearly had me jumping a foot in the air.

"*Miss Darby*," Linus shouted, scaring me half to death as he got far too close to me. At this point, I should be totally used to ghosts just scaring the shit out of me at every available opportunity, but alas, I was not.

I was just glad I didn't have a full bladder or a glass in my hand.

The small boy rushed me, his grayed-out eyes wild. "Miss Darby, you have to come right now. There's a woman. She's hu—"

His words were cut off by a loud pounding at the front door, the banging easily heard from all the way back here. Rather than run through the house, I raced up the back steps and rounded the porch to the front.

Crumpled in a heap at the front door was a small body, while a much bigger one pounded on the wood. Agent Sarina Kenzari listlessly picked her head up from the planks, her bleary gaze chilling me to the bone. At the same time, Jimmy threw the door open, clad only in pajama bottoms and not much else.

"Uncle Dave?" I murmured at the same time Jimmy muttered a nearly silent, "Cap?"

Dave didn't say anything, he just picked Sarina up off the ground and shoved his way into the house. Both Linus and I followed him in, and at the moment, I couldn't give a shit that the ghost was being naughty. I only cared if my friends were okay.

"There better be a medic in this fucking house, Sarina," Dave growled, his voice taking on the animalistic quality of his wolf as he shoved through the front room to the kitchen. The thud of heavy feet rattled down the stairs as the rest of the occupants of the home joined our trek to the kitchen.

"There is," she murmured sleepily, "but we don't have enough time for that. Just give me a gun and put me somewhere safe."

And that's about when I lost it. "Someone needs to tell me what the fuck is going on and *now*."

Dave knocked the fruit bowl from the stone island and dumped Sarina onto it, revealing her bloody shoulder and abdomen, along with his ripped shirt. Four bloody claw marks marred his flesh, sure, but she was so much worse off. One because he was already healing, and two?

Sarina was close enough to death that I could smell it.

"No time," Sarina muttered, her lids sleepy as her head ticked with whatever vision held her sight. "Wolves coming. Followed us. *No time.*"

Shouldering through the crowd, I latched onto her wrist, shoving what little bit of power I had left into her. I didn't have much to spare—not after healing both her and Bishop after Aemon's assault in the graveyard—but I could give her a little bit.

Her face cleared of pain for a second, but her frown was there to stay. "You shouldn't have done that," she whispered, fear coloring her words as her hand latched onto my forearm. "You needed it."

Before she could elaborate, the sound of glass breaking ricocheted through the house. A moment later, several booms rattled the walls as flashes of glaring light damn near blinded us. Without thinking, I slid Sarina off the counter, her half-falling on my lap as I braced my back against the sink.

She shot up, rummaging in the cabinet in front of us before yanking out a black pistol and shoving it into my hands. She could have been talking to me, too, but my ears were toast. I checked the mag and chambered a round before holding out a hand for her to be at my back.

The kitchen was a choke point, the only exit a small window above the sink that I probably couldn't get an ass cheek through. We needed to get the hell out of here. Rounding the island, I spied Yazzie through a cloud of smoke, going toe-to-toe with a gray wolf bigger than any canine had a right to be.

The wolf pounced, launching itself at the agent, and then Yazzie wasn't there anymore. One second the agent appeared to be a moment away from his end, and then in a flash of light and a faint hint of more smoke, there was a fucking Grizzly Bear in the living room. He roared as he swiped at the dog, the vibration rattling my chest as I struggled not to scream myself.

Living on a mountain in Tennessee, I'd seen my fair share of bears, but since I lived in the South and not Montana, my experience stayed on the black bear part of the spectrum. So the six hundred pound bear duking it out with a giant gray wolf not only took up the entirety of the room, but it also had me blinking to make sure I wasn't hallucinating.

Once I was sure I wasn't losing my marbles, I realized I had another dilemma on my hands. Unless I wanted to enter the fray of a wolf-bear death match, my options were limited to running upstairs or going outside. Personally, both options were shit, but outside seemed to be at the worse end of the shit-o-meter.

Those flash-bangs had to have come from somewhere, right?

Yanking Sarina behind me, I pulled us both up the stairs only to stop short. At the landing blocking our way was another wolf. Fangs bared, saliva dripped from its jowls, the pulsation of its growl vibrating my chest, even though I couldn't hear it over the ringing in my ears. Glancing behind me, not only did I get a load of Sarina's petrified face, but also the additional wolf at our backs.

The shifter at the base of the stairs climbed that first step as the one in front of us began its descent. Essentially corralled, there was no other option but to fight our way out.

*What I wouldn't give for a throwing knife right about now.*

There wasn't a whole lot of data about what a bullet would do to the skull of a wolf, but I was damn sure about to find out. Raising my weapon, I fired off two shots before hitting my target, the wolf in front of us seemed to stall mid-leap as it collapsed on the steps beside us. The wolf at our backs charged, and I managed to hit it center mass on our mad dash up the stairs.

My room had weapons—specifically the knives I wanted—I just had to get us there. After that it would all be gravy, right?

Unfortunately, the center mass shot was not quite good enough. A behemoth of a man raced after us, his wolf conspicuously absent as he jumped over his fallen pack mate. Whipping Sarina around me, he caught me mid-tackle, slamming me down to the floor with enough force to have me seeing stars.

My gun went flying as all the air in my lungs waved bye-bye in one big *whoosh*. By the time I could see again, my attacker's claws were descending, heading straight for my face. I rolled, his talons barely missing me as the sound of the world turned back on. A vicious growl filled the hall as a trio of shots rang out. The wolf nearly fell on top of me, but I couldn't complain.

A familiar hand filled my field of vision, and I latched onto J for dear life as he yanked me to standing. Dark hair a mess and sleep shorts barely clinging to his ass, he shoved me behind him as he herded Sarina and I down the hall to my room.

Still catching my breath, I stumbled, nearly knocking into Sarina as we made it to our destination. A warm trickle skittered down my neck, and I reached up to touch the aching mass that was my head. My hand came away red, the blood thick on my fingers.

*That's not good.*

Brain fuzzy, I blinked hard as I struggled not to shake my head. Shaking my head would make this a fuck of a lot worse. Nausea crawled up my throat, but we didn't have time for that shit. Stumbling for my weapons, I passed Sarina a Glock and J an extra mag, while I strapped a dagger to my hip and filled my other hand with throwing knives.

I wasn't exactly sure how accurate I'd be with those blades, but I'd just have to make do with what I had. Trusting myself with a firearm while most likely concussed was stupid and reckless—both adjectives that could be applied to me on a normal basis, but still.

"Where's Dave?" I mumbled. "And Jimmy?"

J gestured to the backyard. "Outside. Come on."

The three of us broke from my room in a single file line, J—the only one of us that wasn't half-dead—taking point. We ran—as much as we were able—back down the stairs. The world swam as J dragged me behind him, and I nearly threw up as the warm wetness trickled down my back, soaking into my shirt.

As we made it to the downstairs landing, the

aftermath of Yazzie's brawl made itself known. Glass and plaster were littered everywhere, mixed liberally with blood and viscera. A wolf's head lay separated from his body, its tongue lolling out, its eyes rolled back in their sockets. But the real fight wasn't in the parlor anymore.

It was outside.

The bellow of a bear rattled what was left of the windows, and J picked up the pace, dragging me far faster than my legs wanted to go. Busting through the back door, I was amazed the National Guard wasn't on our doorstep right now.

Four wolves circled Yazzie, the giant Grizzly swiping at them as they attempted to take the bear down. Acker and Jimmy were also surrounded, two wolves doing their level best to take hunks out of them. Tobin and Dave weren't anywhere to be found, and that worried me far more than it should, considering the bevy of problems in front of us.

J took aim and fired, the bullet knocking one of the wolves off course, while simultaneously making me want to rip my own ears off. The sound rocketed through my brain hard enough to make me stumble. But there was nothing to do about it—Jimmy, Acker, and Yazzie needed our help.

The wolf that J had shot—the one who had nearly

taken a chunk out of Jimmy—now had our little trio in its sights. Moving faster than I thought I could—because concussions were a thing—I had my dagger at the ready, flying down the porch steps at warp speed.

My blade found a home in the fleshy underside of the wolf's jaw, the pointed tip protruding from the top of its head. A pull of nausea filled me as the wolf's eyes rolled back in its skull. Kicking the beast off my blade nearly had me falling to my knees, the ache in my head almost more than I could stand.

A bullet whizzed by my ear, the air displaced enough that I ducked as my head swam. It struck the wolf behind me, the spray of its blood coating my side. But the shot landed wide, not killing the damn thing. Wobbling to my feet, I brought my blade down again, taking the wolf's head as I tried not to toss my cookies.

"*Ambrose*," Linus shouted, the little boy's voice yanking me out of my own bullshit once again. It took far too long for my gaze to find Acker, and by the time I did, it was too late for me to stop the domino from falling.

A wolf latched onto Ambrose's shoulder, its large jaw jerking as it shredded Acker's flesh. It only took a moment, but as soon as Linus saw his living brother in trouble, his form flickered. Pressure popped in my ears as Linus did what I feared he would, his ghostly grayed-out form turning so fast it knocked everyone off their feet.

If I didn't have a concussion before, I sure as shit did now. Peeling myself from the brick pavers, I tried standing, but I couldn't find my feet. All I could do was watch as Linus ripped through wolf after wolf, eviscerating them with the single-minded focus of a child wronged. And if said child happened to be a totally dead thing that could rip whole towns apart, well, then it was a bonus he was on our side.

At least for the time being. As soon as Linus ran out of wolves to kill, he might just start on us.

*Hildy*, I called with my mind. *If you could stop flipping off the queen, I could use an assist.*

Poltergeists were hard to deal with on a good day, and today was not a good day.

"Jesus, Mary, and Joseph," Hildy growled, his voice so welcome I'd almost believed I dreamed it. "I leave ya for a day, and this is what I come back to?"

It was totally wrong that I giggled at that, right? And that it echoed Aemon's words right before he made me take a nap?

Yep. Totally bad.

"A little help, please?" I mumbled, gesturing vaguely

at the very real, very bad ghosty making mincemeat out of a pack of wolves.

Hildy took one look at Linus and his face went soft, the wince there much how I felt. I didn't want Linus to leave, nor did I want him to hurt anyone. But a poltergeist was little better than a rabid dog, and Hildy knew it.

"Poor lad," he murmured, nodding. With a slam of his cane, Hildy held Linus still, but it did little to stop his screams.

*"Ambrose, wake up. Ambrose, please,"* Linus yelled, fighting Hildy's hold. Acker's twin thrashed against Hildy's magic, the smoky green bonds squeezing him tight.

Hildy pulled me up, a feat only possible after he gave me a little of his juice. "Come on, lass. Ya have work to do."

Slowly, I staggered toward Acker, nearly taking a header as I slipped on wolf guts.

"Linus," I called, pitching my voice low. There was a two-fold reason. The first because he needed kindness, and the second? If I spoke any louder, I'd puke. "Can you look at me?"

The boy ignored me at first, still reaching for his brother, even though Hildy's hold was ironclad.

Eventually, he met my gaze. "Ambrose is hurt. You have to save him."

Currently, Acker was being worked on by a bloody Yazzie who was putting pressure on the ragged wound at his shoulder.

"We will, but I need your help." And this is where I felt like the worst person in the world. Because I needed a soul to heal, and I needed a soul to heal Acker, and I needed Linus to move on. Not because I wanted him gone—no, but because he was always too close to the edge, and now that he'd turned, there was nothing else I could do.

"Anything," he breathed, and it took everything I had left in the tank to not start bawling.

"I need you to say goodbye to Ambrose, and then you need to give me a hug."

Linus thrashed, tears welling in his eyes. "But what if he needs me? I did good, right? Those wolves were the bad guys, weren't they?"

Staggering closer, I knelt at Linus' feet. "Oh, sweet boy. You did perfect. But you're solid now, and that can turn bad if you let it. You aren't meant to stay here. If you move on, I'll have enough power to heal your brother."

"Promise?"

"I promise," I whispered, praying I wasn't lying.

"Sloane's waiting for you, you know. And there are tons of kids to play with. You could even say hi to my dad if you want."

His small face lit up for a second before his gaze fell back to his brother. Then he set his shoulders and firmed his mouth, giving me a fierce nod for someone so little. "Okay."

Without a word, Hildy's magic faded, releasing the boy. Linus launched himself at Ambrose, wrapping his now-solid arms around his brother's neck.

"I'm sorry, Ambrose. I'm so sorry," he cried, stuffing his face in Acker's chest.

Acker's beefy arms closed around his brother, a hint of peace threading through the pain on his face. "I forgive you." He choked, squeezing the boy tighter. "And I love you."

Linus pulled back, silvery tears trailing down his face. "Goodbye, brother. I'll miss you."

With that, he ran at me, only this time, I was ready for him. Arms wide, I welcomed Linus' embrace, his soul melting into me as soon as my limbs closed around him. Linus' death had been quick and horrible, his sins so great and so accidental. So preventable.

But Sloane hadn't lied. There was nothing evil about Linus Acker—nothing at all. I had no doubt when he made it to Elysium, she would be waiting for him.

And as usual, Linus' soul healed me, drying up the wound at the back of my head and clearing the fog of impending unconsciousness. As promised, I gave some of that healing to Acker, stemming the flow of blood pouring from his shoulder.

But Linus' soul wasn't enough to heal us all, and I feared the battle wasn't over.

## 17

"What—and I cannot stress this enough —*the fuck* was that?" Yazzie barked, his normally bronze face white as a sheet as he took three steps back.

Confused, I stared at the now-human-shaped shifter like he'd grown another head. "What was what?"

"You weren't bullshitting him about his brother? That was a real ghost that has just been wandering around our house for how long? And who is the guy with the top hat and cane?"

Still not well from what I could only assume was an actual cracked skull, I pinched my brow to try and stave off the headache. "You saw me with the witches, weirdo. You know what I can do. Why would I lie about a ghost in the house?"

"That was before I knew ghosts could do that." Yazzie gestured to the whole of the backyard, covered in wolf residue. "Did you see him just rip through those wolves?"

Considering I was currently sitting in wolf guts, yeah, I totally did. "Don't worry, Yazzie. They're not all like that."

It was a total lie, but he didn't need to know that. Any ghost could turn into a poltergeist if given the right motivation.

Dismissing the shifter, I turned to Hildy. "Thanks for the assist."

"Not that it did much good," he muttered, shaking his head. "You're still a broken-down mess if I ever saw one. You need to call more souls to ya. Get healed up. You know that pack is a lot bigger than just the small bit that attacked here."

Knoxville proper was full of ghosts—a fact I did not like one bit. But Hildy was rarely wrong, and if more wolves were coming, I'd need something better than a cracked skull and fucking pajamas to combat them.

Swallowing hard, I pulled with what little power I had left, calling souls to me that wished to move on. Funnily enough, the first soul was a wolf, the one I'd shot in the head on the stairs. A member of the LeBlanc pack, the man seemed to only be following his alpha's orders. The pack had stormed a building, and he'd been ordered to let no one live. Sarina had escaped and he'd followed, right on to his end.

All ten wolves came to me, not wanting to stay on this plane, no matter what the afterlife meant for them. They raced for me, filling me with their life force as they ran from this earth, as if they knew what was coming and wanted no part of it. As healed and energized as I was after that, their trepidation made the nausea return.

Granted, it could be the backyard full of wolf guts, but I was pretty sure the fear was what did it.

Uneasy, I healed Acker first, making good on my promise to his brother before moving on to everyone else who was supremely fucked up after a sunrise wolf attack.

By the time I got to Sarina, Dave and Tobin emerged from the house. Both were awfully bloody, a red smear smudging a lens of Tobin's glasses. Tobin was half-holding Dave up, the bigger man too much for him to carry.

"I'm going to heal you all up, but someone had better start talking, and now," I growled, pressing a glowing hand to Dave's bloody abdomen.

The gray mist that had flowed from my hands a few days ago now had a golden quality to it, the lack of Aemon's presence in my body changing my powers yet again. It worried me that I didn't know what had been him and what had been me—especially in that wolf challenge at the pack house. With Azrael's last gift, I had no idea what I could actually do now, though, if I had a guess, the insta-healing myself part wasn't in my wheelhouse anymore.

"You tell her," Sarina grumbled, lifting her chin at Dave. "I'm still bound by that stupid oath."

Still being a member of the ABI, Sarina was obligated to keep their secrets under threat of death. To even consider breaking their confidence would bring a whole lot of pain to her doorstep.

Dave snorted as he wilted to the porch planks, letting my healing touch ease his pain. "Do you want the long story or the short one?"

"That depends on if there are any more wolves about to break down the door," I snapped, irritated that he was stalling at all. My dad's favorite concert T-shirt was now covered in wolf blood for fuck's sake.

"After the bullshit at the pack house, I decided keeping an eye on my father's pack seemed like a really good idea," Dave began. "Took some time off, thought it wouldn't take too long for them to start some shit."

Funny, we had, too. I shot a look at Yazzie, and he gave me a small shake of his head.

"I tracked them to a building up in Ascension, on the

outskirts. A warehouse that had once been a paper mill. My guess is it's some kind of black site so they can do shady shit outside of Knoxville."

As soon as he said the words "black site," a sinking feeling in my gut yawned wide open into a pit of dread. "You'd better not say what I think you're gonna. Do not tell me that man is free. Do not tell me those wolves helped him. Don't you fucking dare."

Sloane had been right all along, hadn't she? She'd known she should have just killed Essex—she did—but she stopped to save my ass, and now where were we? Right here with him out and people dead. Those wolves hadn't wanted to kill us, but they'd been bound by their alpha to do so—the magic forcing them to follow orders. And how many people died at the warehouse?

She should have killed him when she had the chance.

"Are you fucking kidding me?" Hildy railed, popping in solid once again and scaring Yazzie half to death. "Your da's pack helped Essex Drake escape?"

Dave's reaction to Hildy just becoming solid would have been worth it under any other circumstances, but right now? I just wanted to rage.

Audibly gulping, Dave's dark skin turned gray as he stared at my ghostly yet solid grandfather. "I'm sorry, Darby. But I believe that's exactly what they did."

Instead of screaming my head off, I waved for him to

continue—the glow of my hands now at surface-of-the-sun levels.

"I saw Sarina running with wolves on her ass, so I helped her out. We ran all night, making it here after almost losing them twice. But our lead was too short. I'm sorry. We just didn't know where else to go."

That softened me. For the first time in maybe ever, Dave had come to me for help instead of the other way around. "You did the right thing—as long as we aren't all going to be carted off to human jail, that is. Someone is going to call the cops around here, right? I mean, those flash-bangs weren't exactly quiet."

"Umm, sweetie," Sarina said, giving me a small grimace, "you're on the arcane side of town and you're the Warden. You *are* the police. Nobody—and I do mean *nobody*—is calling anyone. Though, the 'welcome to the neighborhood' is going to get a little awkward."

Stopping to listen, I noted the complete absence of sirens, which was a good thing, considering the level of wolf entrails just coating everything. There would have been no way at all to explain this shit, and I doubted there was a strong enough glamour in the world to hide what was going on out here.

Nodding, I surveyed the courtyard, wishing for a hose or something. Or a magic wand that could make this shit go away.

Essex was free. He was free. All the safety I'd had with him locked up was just... gone.

A hand at my shoulder had me looking up into Jimmy's pale eyes. "Go take a shower. We've got this." He gestured to the lawn full of eviscerated wolf. "Take a beat, and then we'll fix it, yeah?"

Hildy nodded. "Listen to the elf. Get yerself sorted, and then we can find that weaselly bastard. And this time, no one is handing him off. He'll meet his end even if I have to do it myself."

My chuckle was dark, but I was grateful, nonetheless.

By the time I washed the blood out of my hair and clothes, the reality of what happened hit me. This had me calling Thomas for the second time in a single day as I furiously dressed.

"What?" he answered, only this time, I didn't give him shit.

"He's out," I whispered, unable to make my voice go any louder as I threw a trio of blessed rosaries over my head.

Essex Drake had hurt us all—nearly killing half the Night Watch in one fell swoop. He'd murdered Sloane's parents. His actions had gotten my father killed. Hell, he'd wielded the blade that had killed Azrael himself.

And none of that took into account all the siblings he'd slaughtered. His hands were so bloody, it was a wonder they weren't dripping.

"I know," he barked, his frustration rattling down the line. "Simon and Axel are already out looking for him. Soon, the rest of us will be, too. Every agency in a thousand-mile radius is on this. That secure black site Davenport went on and on about? Didn't just hold your brother. I swear, if I get ahold of those wolves…"

He didn't need to finish that sentence. Ingrid was right. They should have killed them fifty years ago—or at the very least, their alpha. I'd rectify that shit posthaste.

"Good. I'll see you out there," I said, seating my gun back in its holster. "But watch your back. Those wolves? They aren't playing nice."

Thomas' laugh was one-part glee and one-part pure hatred. "I bet they aren't. Funny, I won't be playing nice, either. And Darby?"

"Yeah?" I asked, fitting a trio of throwing knives into my boot.

"No more deals," he ordered, and I couldn't help but agree with him. Though, it hadn't been me who'd made the deal with Davenport in the first place. It had been Sloane. "This shit ends."

"That's the plan," I murmured before hanging up.

And this time I wouldn't be worried about Bishop going to jail or pardons for my friends.

Essex Drake was going to die, and anyone that helped him escape was going to meet the end of my blade.

Fuck the ABI.

Fuck the council.

Fuck that bullshit wolf pack.

Hastily braiding my hair into a tail, I made my way downstairs to look for my resident shifter expert, barely noticing the lack of blood and bodies. He'd been in charge of surveilling the wolves, and we'd not heard one word about them leaving the compound, let alone amassing enough people to raid an ABI black site.

Finding the shifter in the kitchen, I raised a singular eyebrow and waited. If I said a word, I'd yell my freaking head off, and Yazzie didn't deserve that.

Probably.

Gritting his teeth, he slid the phone over to me. "I went through the feeds. There's nothing. No movement, not a single wolf leaving the den." He yanked on the end of his own braid—his frustration clear. "I swear, I would have told you."

I stared at the screens full of wolf activity, but Yazzie was right. No one had left the compound—not where the cameras could see.

"Did you get the catacombs?" Sarina asked, breezing into the room as she towel-dried her short black bob.

*Shit.*

There had been tunnels under the Dubois cathedral as well, and who had owned the church before the vampires?

The fucking LeBlanc pack.

It made sense that every property would have those same damn tunnels. No wonder the cameras hadn't picked up the pack's movements, and why those damn wolves didn't so much as flinch as Yazzie put them up.

Hell, those wolves had probably seen him do it.

I met Yazzie's gaze, his just as tight with shame as mine was with rage.

"Son of a bitch," he groaned, leaning down to thump his head against the counter. "No wonder. I can't believe I got fooled by a bunch of mangy pieces of—"

"That's enough," Dave growled, pulling a fresh black T-shirt down his stomach. "We need a plan. One that doesn't start with me losing my best friend's kid to a wolf massacre."

"Oh, I have a plan, all right," I replied. "But I doubt you're going to like it."

But unless we wanted to kill everyone, I didn't think there was another option left. Those wolves hadn't wanted to kill, nor had they wanted to attack this house or the warehouse. They'd begged for peace, only to be forced under a tyrant's thumb.

Sarina's gaze got a far-off quality to it as if she was looking at something in the distance. She blinked back to herself, shaking her head. "I think your Omega days are numbered."

Dave gripped the counter, his hold tight enough that the stone hissed in protest. I couldn't exactly blame the man. As the last heir to the LeBlanc line, he was likely the only person strong enough to go against his father—the only one able to resist the alpha's magic. As an Omega, Dave didn't have a pack—didn't have an alpha—and for damn sure didn't want one.

But unless we wanted hundreds of dead wolves on our hands, it was a mantle he'd have to take.

"Is it the only way?" he asked Sarina, his voice as hopeful as I'd ever heard it.

She winced in answer. "No, but it is the only way that will let you sleep at night."

Dave swallowed, closing his eyes. "Then get me in there. I'll do the rest."

Resting my hand on his, I squeezed. Storming the catacombs was the dumbest idea yet, but I feared it was the only one we had left.

## 18

"Please tell me you aren't this dumb," a small childlike voice chastised, the hissed whisper a surprise since I should have been alone.

For once I didn't even flinch, too busy staring through a scope down the barrel of a rifle, aimed at a wolf's head. I had no intention of taking the shot, but I needed the lay of the land before I called anyone else in. Peeling my gaze from the wolf in my sites, I shot a glare at Ingrid.

"This has to be the dumbest fucking plan I've ever heard of, and considering you've had some doozies over the years, that's saying something," Ingrid griped, her voice pitched low so as to not alert the teaming fucking pack of wolves in the valley below.

She wasn't wrong exactly. My plan lacked a certain

level of well, *planning*. Especially since it all hinged on A: finding the LeBlanc Alpha, and B: not dying before Dave got to him. But this was the most direct way to suss out Essex's location and stop him for good. Plus, we needed to nip Cassius LeBlanc's reign of terror before it got worse.

My gaze strayed to Hildy who was inspecting his nails and pointedly *not* looking at me. He was staunchly against this course of action, and he'd made his position known. Repeatedly. If I had a guess, either Sarina or Hildy himself had been the one to tattle.

I returned my left eye to the scope, ignoring Ingrid and her three friends. Björn stood by my friend's side, crouched low and scanning for threats. Her two other companions seemed familiar, but I didn't pay much attention to them, too busy staring at a stupid wolf lick his paw when he was supposed to be guarding the entrance to the catacombs.

"You got a better idea?" I murmured, scanning the horizon for the wolf's friends.

Grumbling, she gave me a begrudging "no" before crouching in the grass next to me. It was the same answer I'd gotten from Hildy, but he'd added that he didn't have a better idea because he at least had three brain cells to rub together.

"Then maybe shut up? Or offer assistance? Or

something else besides telling me I'm stupid. I get it. I'm supposed to be on the trail of a big, bad demon, but I'm more worried about Essex than I am Aemon. Out of the two, my brother has far more blood on his hands."

One of Ingrid's companions started giggling—like actually giggling as if he was a ten-year-old girl at a slumber party. "Ooh, I knew I liked you. At every turn it's as if you don't have a lick of survival instincts, but you just won't die. And heading into a swarm of wolves without so much as a strategy? Darling, if this were a TV show, I'd be cheering you on, you little underdog you."

I remembered Ingrid's friends now. The idiot babbling on and on about my stupidity was Grape Guy from the council, and the man beside him rolling his eyes had to be his seatmate.

"I mean, I'm going to survive this, but you?" He reclined to rest his head in the spot of shade. "*Sweetie*. If you make it out of this, it'll be a miracle."

Ingrid slapped Grape Guy upside the head, tousling his auburn hair. "Shut up, Kato. I'm trying to convince her to think this through, not practically dare her to do it, you idiot."

But Ingrid didn't have to go through the trouble. I only had to find a way into the caves without alerting the rest of the pack, and everything would go to plan. Probably.

"Personally," Kato's friend began, "I think it's a good idea. If they have a better candidate for Alpha, then taking out LeBlanc is the easiest way to bring the whole pack down without a massive loss of life. The fact that he's still Alpha at all is a detriment to the whole species. If he keeps on this path, someone will eliminate the whole line, and they won't care too much about the people they kill along the way."

Kato rolled his eyes. "Leave it to Reynard to spout some bullshit wisdom." He rotated in the grass to his belly, resting his chin on his fists. "Tell me—are all druids so painfully boring, or is it just you?"

Reynard shot him a glare. "It's all of us."

That's when I'd decided I'd had enough. "If you aren't helping, I'm going to need you to get the fuck out of here. I have shit to do and not a lot of time to do it."

Phase one of my plan was about to roll into motion, just as soon as the guard shift changed. There was a rather bored-looking wolf licking his paw at the mouth of an entrance, but farther down the hill, a whole slew of his pack mates were lazing in the sun. When the guards changed position, I planned on sneaking everyone but J into the cave.

I still hadn't thought of exactly what I wanted to do with J, but no part of me wanted him going into the catacombs with us. Because this was worse than when he strolled into the Dubois nest with me or when he'd been kidnapped by ghouls. This was as Ingrid said, "The dumbest fucking plan ever" and if I didn't make it out, I wanted him safe. J was the last piece of my family, the last bit of my sanity, and I just couldn't lose him.

"You manage to talk her out of it?" the man in question asked, irritation clear in his tone.

He wasn't supposed to be this close. Hell, he was supposed to be a mile up the mountain, convincing Jimmy to make him a protection necklace like I'd told him to.

"No, she's being stubborn," Ingrid replied as if I couldn't hear them. "Unfortunately, she's also right—especially about your involvement. You shouldn't be here."

"She's my partner—"

"Shut. Up," Ingrid growled, cutting J off. "You are one of the last people she loves, you idiot. What happens if you don't make it out of here, hmm? Forget about your foolish male ego. What will it do to her?"

I lifted my gaze from the scope to stare at J. Jeremiah had been my best friend—my brother—for most of my life. If anything happened to him, I'd never be able to forgive myself. And it wouldn't matter if it was my fault or not or if he made the decision to stay. I would own it regardless.

But J wasn't looking at Ingrid. No, he was staring at me. "Nothing is going to happen to me."

"You don't know that," I hissed. "Forget about me. What about Jimmy? What about the life you have, your family?"

If Mrs. Cooper knew what we were doing…

I didn't have much of either anymore, but J? He had everything in front of him. And as good as it felt to have that connection to my old life—to have the memories and the love—he didn't belong with me anymore.

And reeling him back in? Well, it was about the most selfish thing I could do.

"Please go home. Please?"

J's jaw tightened in defiance. "No, D. I don't trust anyone else to watch your back but me. I helped at the house, didn't I?"

He had. If he hadn't been there, well, whether or not we were infiltrating the wolf den wouldn't be a question, now, would it? He'd saved my ass, watched my six, and kept his cool.

"Yeah," I admitted, my throat clogged. "Yeah, you did."

"Oh, enough of this horse shit," Ingrid growled. "I want your consent. Right here and right now."

J stumbled back a step. "For what?"

My small blonde friend jabbed her finger in J's chest.

"You know damn well what I'm talking about. You have two choices, Cooper. You go home where it's safe, or you give me your consent to turn you if there is no other way. Mags would have just turned you and damn the consequences, but that's not my style."

The implications of that statement hit me somewhere in my gut. She was giving him a choice because she never got one, and the thought made me sick. Just fuck Nero. Fuck him sideways with a rusty chainsaw.

"So pick one," she hissed, jabbing her finger in his chest once more. "Just know, you step one toe in that cave, and I'm choosing for you, got it?"

J contemplated Ingrid in her little girl jeans and hoodie, her hair in braids and her feet in sparkly tennis shoes. She would fit in at a third-grade class better than she did here, but she was the oldest of all of us.

"Your queen gave me the same ultimatum a month ago," he replied, narrowing his eyes at her. "She didn't have to make good on it and neither will you. But if it comes down to it, I expect you to do whatever it is you think you have to do."

That wasn't an answer, but it was the best we were going to get. J had never been comfortable with the arcane world. In fact, had I not dragged him into it, he would have been happier not knowing this side of the world existed.

Or at least he used to.

Now, though, I didn't know how he felt, other than he wanted to have my back. And that I could respect.

"Fair enough, but remember what I said." Ingrid's gaze was sharp on my best friend. It didn't matter that she was in a child's body—forever underestimated, forever frozen—she was stronger than any of us could possibly fathom, and she meant business.

"I'll remember," J murmured, meeting my gaze for a moment before mine skittered away to stare down the barrel once more.

"Oh, this is all just so touching," Kato cooed, and I had to fight off the urge to kick him. But at his grunt, someone had clearly beat me to it.

"Stop being an asshole," Reynard grumbled. "Not all of us can just turn into a beetle or some other such nonsense and scurry away. For some of us, this is actually dangerous."

It just figured Kato was a shifter.

Soon, the one thing I'd been waiting for finally happened. The majority of the wolves started migrating south, and the lone pack member at the entrance to the cave began his descent to the valley. If I was right, we had twenty minutes—*tops*—to get inside those catacombs to infiltrate the LeBlanc pack.

Twenty minutes.

Plenty of time.

It turned out twenty minutes was more than enough time to get a shifter, a bound Mormo, a mage uninherit, a wolf, and an elf down the mountain. The bigger problem was making sure Tobin didn't fall face-first down the slope and accidentally kill himself.

The comms specialist was awkward with his shotgun to say the least, but Dave vouched for him, informing us all that he'd be dead if it weren't for the mousey agent. Evidently, Tobin utilized every first-person shooter game ever made and was actually a good shot. As long as he stayed in between Yazzie and Acker, I didn't care what he did as long as he didn't end up dead.

Our gaggle of twelve—*plus Hildy*—made our way to the entrance, the shifters of the group not bothering to change as we entered enemy territory. I trusted the vampires noses enough to not want to deal with talking to an animal—especially with such a mixed group.

"Remember the name of the game, ladies and gents," I murmured once we were a few steps inside. "The goal is getting Dave to Cassius LeBlanc. He'll take it from there. Protect Dave, keep him safe. Got it?"

I got a few nods, a few smiles, and one sarcastic bow from Kato. I'd just have to take it.

But the wide mouth of the entrance did not prepare us for the hazards of the catacombs themselves.

Not one bit.

## 19

Unlike the Dubois nest catacombs, the ones under the LeBlanc pack house were rougher, newer. The craggy walls seemed hewn only months ago, the fragile supports ready to collapse at any moment.

So they hadn't just come back to Knoxville a week ago.

They'd slowly but surely dug their way through a fucking mountain to recapture their former home—their meticulous actions those of a solid plan rather than a circumstance of fate. They'd been ready to make their mark on Knoxville—ready to take it if need be.

It made sense that they'd aligned themselves with Essex. My brother was nothing if not methodical—

always having a backup plan. Hell, he had a backup to the backup, but I wondered if in all his careful planning he ever saw Sloane coming. Because eventually, she would be coming for him.

And when she did, there would be no escaping her. Now all we needed was for Dave to take over, and these wolves would have no choice but to tell us where they'd hidden my brother.

It would be faster than searching—if we lived long enough.

The problem with catacombs? Too many damn tunnels.

Sarina led us through the first fork, her second sight showing the way, but once we got to the next one? Well, let's just say there were too many variables.

Grabbing her hand, I gave it a little squeeze. "I know it's a lot, but—"

She turned her chin to me, but her eyes stayed glued to the dark tunnels that led through the soft limestone mountain. "I don't know." She pointed to the tunnel farthest to the right. "That one is where a small pack family lives part-time. The children are sleeping. Young pups. The one beside it? Older wolves. Elderly. Close to death. Won't live past the year." She moved onto the next. "Thirty-somethings. One of the females is pregnant with her first. She's in human form but the father is in his wolf, protecting her. She's going to lose the baby soon. Chromosomal defect. He can smell it." She shook her head, squeezing her eyes shut.

"Okay," I cooed, rubbing her arms. What had Bishop done when Sarina was freaking out? Lead her through the visions, right? I could do that. "Cast aside the ancillary. Try to find the path to the alpha. Think of Cassius. Picture him in your mind. Find the thread that leads to him."

She squinted in the dim, the faint light from the wall torches barely reaching us. Shaking her head once more, she pointed to the far tunnel and the third from the left.

"We have to split up." But the way she said it, she didn't think this was the right answer, either. "If we all go, we all die," she whispered, her words barely audible except for those closest to her. "Choke point. Many wolves," she muttered, gesturing to the far-left tunnel. "Have to hold them back so the rest don't get through."

Ingrid's smile flashed in the dim light as she pulled a wicked blade from the inside of her little girl hoodie. "That sounds like a job for me." She nodded to Björn. "You coming?"

"What part of our queen's 'stay out of trouble' decree is a mystery to you?" Björn muttered, shaking his head as he massaged his temple.

"Probably the 'out' part?" Ingrid replied, her smile

that of a mercurial child who just wanted to see her caretaker break. "Remember that section of reality where *I'm* in charge of *her* safety and not the other way around? Just because I look like a child doesn't mean I am one." She began skipping toward the "danger" tunnel. "Come on, Sonny Jim. Let me show you what us old girls can do."

Reynard pivoted on a heel to follow them, making the knot in my gut ease just a little. Then he shot a blue ball of magic at Kato, smacking him upside the head. "Come on, you flaming sack of elephant shit. We have a job to do."

Kato seemed to pout, wanting to stay with our little huddle, but he ruefully clomped over with the other ancients, dragging his feet the whole time. Maybe he wanted to see me do more stupid shit. Maybe he needed the entertainment in his life. Or maybe he knew something we didn't.

My gaze found Yazzie's, and I canted my head in Ingrid's direction. Nodding, he grabbed Acker and Tobin's collars and dragged them in the vampire's wake.

"We need to go that way," Sarina pleaded, pointing to the third from the left opening as her gaze seemed to cloud over.

Hildy met my eyes over her head, his jaw tight. "I don't like this. Something isn't right. I can smell it."

None of this was right. Sure, I'd wanted to waltz in here, slit the alpha's throat, and call it good. But the longer we went without seeing wolves meant they had to be somewhere, and I didn't like that we could get trapped down here with no way out. I flicked my eyes to the tunnel and back to him, silently asking for his help.

"Sure thing, lass," he muttered, giving me a nod before he zoomed toward the path we were contemplating going through. A moment later he appeared at the mouth of it, waving for us to continue. "Seems clear enough, but keep a weather eye out."

Dave and I took point with J and Sarina in the middle and Jimmy bringing up the rear, entering the tunnel on silent feet and more trepidation than I could swallow. Eschewing my gun, I drew the dagger at my hip, trying to ready myself for whatever it was that Sarina was seeing.

"This way, lass." Hildy guided in the now-pitch-black passageway, the light from the torches not reaching us here. Granted, Dave and I could still see just fine, but the only light to be had emanated from my ghostly grandfather—a light only I could see.

I grabbed J's hand and put it on my shoulder, leading him farther into the darkness as I traversed the rough cave floor, picking my way around rocks and mounds of dirt. This part of the cave was rougher than the entrance, rockier, and if it weren't for the gated offshoots with their steel bars and thick locks, I would have assumed it was a natural part of the landscape.

J stumbled over a large rock, knocking into me and sending us rolling down a sharp decline on the path. No matter how hard you tried, falling was never quiet. And falling with a blade in one's hand also required a certain level of finesse that meant silence wasn't exactly on the menu.

We landed in a heap, my dagger clattering to the rocky ground with an echoing clang of metal on stone. Then everything seemed to happen at once.

Each one of the gated tunnel offshoots opened, the bars rising into the limestone as if they were on a timer. Their ratcheting clanks reverberated through the stone walls, and I pushed myself to my feet, yanking J up behind me. Wolves poured from those narrow paths, flowing like water into the main tunnel, their growls and snaps making them seem larger, fiercer, deadlier somehow.

And it wasn't one or two. No, it was more like fifty.

I hadn't fared so well without Aemon's power against a single wolf, and I wanted no part of a gaggle that big.

"*Move*," Dave roared, latching onto my shoulder as he ran deeper into the belly of the beast.

As we moved, I raced toward my downed dagger and

scooped it up, dragging J behind me and praying he didn't fall. I couldn't see Jimmy or Sarina, but I hoped they were following us. But the deeper we ran into the cave, the more of those offshoots opened, practically pouring wolves into the tunnel.

Blindly, I cast out the power I'd gained from their brethren, the gold misting fog seeming to carry a physical weight. Slamming it into the closest dogs, I shoved them back as we raced deeper and deeper into the den. Several wolves leapt over their downed brothers, not stopping as they trampled over them to get to us.

A blaze of magic winked at me from farther down the tunnel, glittering gold orbs slamming into the horde as the echo of gunshots ricocheted through the enclosed space.

*Jimmy and Sarina.*

A sea of wolves teemed between us, too many for us to fight as more seemed to pour into the tunnel. I slammed my power into them as I slashed with my dagger. I didn't want to kill these wolves, but wanting didn't make the necessity go away. Guilt clawed at me as I took a wolf's head, but it didn't stop my blade, the buzz of his soul leaving his body compounding the ache in my chest.

J took several shots, the suppressor on his weapon

doing fuck all to muffle the concussion in such a small space. Ears ringing, head aching, I tried to shove as many wolves back as I could. When he ran out of bullets, J yanked my other dagger from its sheath, hacking right alongside me.

But there were just too many for me to hold that way, too many wolves that would trample their family on their alpha's orders. A wolf sailed past my magic, its huge paws knocking into me. Hell, it felt like I'd been hit by a freight train. Claws ripped into my shoulder, through the leather jacket, and catching on the rosaries at my neck.

Beads spilled and clattered to the ground as blood pulsed from the wound, its giant snout snapping at my face. I rolled, slashing with the blade as the wound closed on its own. The edge of my dagger sliced into its neck—too shallow to kill, but enough to make it rethink its attack. Before it could maneuver another strike, I shoved the blade into its eye.

I didn't wait for the wolf's soul to make a decision—I scooped it up, absorbing it as fast as I could. Power shot out of me, slamming the wolves back as J ran past.

Over the echoes of growls and snaps and barks, a deep, booming laugh overtook it all as a litany of torches blazed at once. I searched the tunnel for Dave, but only J stood between me and the wolf alpha.

"You thought you could come in here and none of us would notice?" Cassius LeBlanc said once his mirth died down. "Stand down," he growled, his eyes glowing blue with his power. "I want her to hear me."

Instantly, the wolves I'd been holding back quieted, no longer pushing at what little power I had left.

My smile was bitter as I met the alpha's gaze. "Oh, I knew you'd notice. But you see, you have something I want—or rather *someone*. Now, I've worked real hard putting my asshole of a brother behind bars, and you just up and set him free. You thought you and I had problems before?" My chuckle was malevolent. "Well, this is a whole other matter."

A familiar wolf padded from the shadows, his steel-gray coat gleaming in the light of the torches as he approached the alpha. One step, and he was a wolf, and the next, Dave stood on two legs in front of his father.

LeBlanc appeared surprised that his son could defy his order to stand down, but this was exactly what I'd hoped for—what Dave was so scared wouldn't work. No, Dave didn't have a pack as an Omega, but his father's blood still ran through his veins.

His father's Alpha blood which held so much power over his wolves.

But the surprise on Cassius' face then was nothing

224 | ANNIE ANDERSON

compared to the utter shock that overtook him at what Dave said next.

"Cassius LeBlanc, I challenge you for your position as Alpha."

## 20

"An Omega is going to challenge me? A half-breed?" Cassius' laugh boomed through the cavern once again. "I don't think so."

Dave's smile was feral, his once-brown irises glowing with the same blue light that his father had. "As decreed by your sacred oath as Alpha, you are bound to accept any challenge to your throne. You scared you won't win?"

Cassius' mouth curled into a simpering smile. "Are you?"

Dave didn't say another word. Instead, he leapt to his wolf form, ending the posturing. Uncle Dave had never been one to mince words, and his phase seemed like one giant "fuck you" to his father.

"I guess not," the alpha muttered, his pitying smile

not leaving his son. He shook his head, his mouth pulled in mock chagrin. "Don't say I didn't warn you." And right before he jumped to his wolf, the alpha bellowed one last order: "*Attack.*"

The wolves that had been quiet, the ones no longer pressing on my power, jumped up in full force. At their alpha's challenge, the horde as a whole shoved against me with a renewed weight.

It didn't matter that the alpha's order was against the covenant. It didn't matter that it was against the rules of an alpha challenge or that his desperate plea for help undermined his rule. Cassius LeBlanc was a weak, tired old man, futilely holding onto a title he should have surrendered decades ago. His wolves obeyed anyway, heaving against my wilting power with the force of hundreds.

Staggering, I pushed harder, my legs wobbling beneath me before a wolf broke free. Leaping past my meager shield, the animal barreled toward me with its too-fast speed and laser-precise aim. Jowls dripping with saliva, it bounded at me before it took to the air once more, teeth and claws at the ready.

A flash of silver raked across its belly, and the wolf fell, sliding with now-dead weight against the rough cave floor. J's dagger was now red with its blood, and without missing a beat, he jabbed the blade into its neck and twisted. Gratefully, I yanked at the soul pulling free of her body, taking it into myself before my power could die.

But my shield was weakened, the wolves too many, too strong. Sweat dripped down my face as I tried to hold it, but that one soul just wasn't enough. A great bellow reached my ears from deeper in the cave, as a swath of glittering gold and green magic bowled through the dogs, knocking them off their feet. My power flickered and died, the magic knocking me, too, on my ass.

A moment later, Jimmy marched through the lot of them, sword in one hand with Sarina under his other arm, and Hildy bringing up the rear. Both of the living were bloody, half-stumbling, the pair of them picking through the scattered wolves and collapsing onto the dirt. Hildy, however, seemed like he was having a good old time, sauntering through the tunnel like he was on vacation.

*Good of him to show up.*

"You sure know how to throw a party, lass," Hildy muttered, cringing once he got a good look at me. "Sorry for abandoning ya. These two needed the help."

Given that Sarina and Jimmy were among the living, I couldn't exactly be mad, but I was about out of goodwill for a while.

Sarina fell to her back, her breathing labored, while Jimmy crawled to J and cupped his face in his hands. His breath heavy, he pressed his forehead to my best friend's before laying a searing kiss on his lips. Renewed, Jimmy let his power free again, only his was a lot bigger and better than mine, adding to my magic and shutting out the rousing pack from the real battle.

Two wolves circled each other—both shades of gray, both huge, but one was just a touch taller, a bit wider, a bit lighter. The bigger one swiped at the smaller—a silly feint that had the smaller, darker one shuffling back. As soon as it took the bait, the bigger one charged, fangs and claws at the ready as it tried to take out the smaller one's flank.

The smaller of the wolves twisted, playing "Keep Away" with its soft underbelly as it went for the larger ones back leg. The snap of its jaws breaking the bone had me covering my face with my hands, praying that it wasn't Dave with a broken leg. The injured wolf howled, the pained cry echoing through the cavern as the rousing wolves behind us beat at Jimmy's ward.

But the smaller wolf didn't stop there. It raked its claws across the white pelt covering its belly. The soft white fur bled to scarlet as the magic protecting us from certain death flickered. I pulled from the deepest part of me, calling for whatever souls I could—just in case.

But I was too late.

A member of the LeBlanc pack pried themselves free of Jimmy's magic, racing for the alpha's challenge. It leapt onto the soon-to-be victor's back just as he was about to clamp down on the loser's neck. The victor shrugged the attacker off, slamming it into the cave wall. The bigger wolf tried to pry himself from the floor, but its back leg wouldn't hold it.

The smaller wolf didn't waste any time charging, and in an instant, the larger wolf's throat was gone, the blue glowing light in its eyes dying.

I couldn't tear my eyes from the challenge—even as the pressure on my and Jimmy's barrier intensified—not until I knew who won.

Not until I knew if Dave was alive.

As soon as the loser was gone, the winner's howl rent the air, reverberating off the cave walls as if it was unmaking the world. The wolves froze before each and every one bowed their heads and crouched to the cave floor.

This was it. If the winning wolf wasn't Dave, we wouldn't make it out of here. It didn't matter how much magic Jimmy and I had or how much help Hildy could give us.

Pulling the last of my power back, I shot a worried glance in Sarina's direction, praying she'd tell me good news. Instead of the smile I wanted, she tipped her chin at the alpha. A moment later, Dave once again stood on two feet, and I wilted to my ass in the dirt.

Tears filled my eyes as relief hit me. This was the dumbest of dumb plans—the absolute worst idea I'd ever had in my life—but I was so fucking happy it worked. Swallowing the spent fear down, I gritted my teeth against the sobs that wanted to claw their way up my throat.

"You all are here as witnesses to Cassius LeBlanc's demise," Dave commanded, his voice carrying, even though he wasn't yelling. "I have won the challenge for Alpha of this pack. All who wish to leave, do so now or face the consequences. All challenges will be honored."

Not a single wolf behind me moved—each one staying right where they were.

That had to be a good sign, right?

But as soon as that thought crossed my brain, naturally, shit had to go sideways.

"I challenge you," a man growled from his hands and knees, his French accent thick. He was the wolf Dave had thrown off his back in the middle of the last alpha challenge, his human form a mid-sized male with longish hair, thick beard, and heavy motorcycle jacket. The dark-headed man climbed to his feet as he wiped blood from his lip.

"He's dead, Emile," Dave murmured softly. "You don't have to do this. He can't hurt you anymore." But Emile only growled in response.

Dave nodded in acceptance, a sad frown marring his face. "So be it."

Emile ran for Dave, shifting on the fly, but the new alpha was far too fast for him. Dave caught him by the throat midair, snapping his neck with unemotional and efficient grace. Before Emile's body hit the ground, Dave had phased back, his face made of stone.

"Anyone else?" Dave boomed, threading power into his voice as it fell over us all. When no one came forward, he tipped up his chin. "Rise."

Each of the wolves got to their feet, phasing back.

Dave surveyed them, his once-dark eyes shining with the blue alpha light—of his wolf. "Answer one question, and then you may attend to your dead. Where is Essex Drake?"

Murmurs rent the crowd, but no one stepped forward until a small teenage boy shuffled through the group. He hesitantly approached, bowing his head to his new alpha as he got closer, his clothes billowing on his emaciated frame. "Umm, I don't mean to disrespect you here, Sir, but—"

Dave reached for the boy's shoulder, and the teen flinched back before he could touch him.

"Easy," Dave murmured. "I'm not going to hurt you. I just want you to look at me."

The teen hesitantly raised his head but refused to look Dave in the eye. "Again, no disrespect here, but wh-who is Essex Drake?"

My heart dropped to my feet as the implications of the kid's questions hit.

Did we get it wrong?

Did they not know who they'd freed?

Was Cassius LeBlanc keeping his pack in the dark?

I couldn't keep my mouth shut. "Your pack freed him last night," I accused, my voice wobbling just as much as my legs were. "Stormed an ABI black site and set a murderer free. I want to know where he is. Now."

The kid blinked at me before hiding behind Dave. Yeah, my hands were glowing. Yeah, I was mad. But after what they'd done, who could blame me?

He peeked around his new alpha. "Do-does he have white hair like you?"

*So they had seen him.* "Yeah, bud, he does. Pinched face, snooty voice, typically wearing a suit. Ring any bells?"

The kid nodded his head vigorously and pointed a trembling arm at the tunnel behind him. "I saw two men head that way today. One of them had white hair like yours." He seemed to gather himself, standing taller.

"We didn't know—most of us, anyway. And the ones who did? We couldn't disobey. We're not bad people," he insisted. "We've just had sh-shitty leaders." His gaze fell to my feet as he ducked behind Dave again.

*Fair enough.* Pursing my lips, I gave the kid a jerky nod. He was right—their free will had been taken from them. I'd seen it myself.

But who knew if Essex was still here or if his backup had stood down? I directed my attention to my best friend. "Stay here with Dave," I insisted, holding out my hand for my other dagger. "Make sure the others are okay. Deal?"

J seemed affronted. "Who's going to watch your six?"

Narrowing my eyes at him, I snatched the dagger from his hand as I fished two extra mags out of the sleeve in my boot. "You are, you stubborn bastard."

He held his arms wide. "Out of the two of us, which one isn't falling down?"

Again, he wasn't wrong. He'd saved my ass, and there was no one else I wanted at my back but him.

Shifting to face Hildy, I transferred my order to my ghostly grandfather. "Find Ingrid and the rest. Make sure they're okay?"

Hildy grumbled something about stubborn grandchildren before his skull cane alighted with his green magic. He latched onto my shoulder, easing my aches and steadying my feet. "I don't like this one bit, lass. We got lucky. You'd better draw on the souls left. Take Cassius if need be. I don't care if the bastard feels like poison. Essex Drake is no one to be messed with unarmed."

Closing my eyes, I drew on that sense, that power that called to the dead. But out of all the souls that filled me, Cassius LeBlanc was not one of them. Pity. I would have loved to know why he'd aligned himself with my brother. Hell, I'd love to know if those fires that killed all those people had been his idea.

As juiced up as I was going to get, I opened my eyes, gave Hildy a nod and marched into another unknown, J and Jimmy at my heels. At least this time, when I tromped through the tunnel, it was lit with torches so my best friend didn't trip.

Several minutes later, we came to a sort of antechamber as the narrow mouth of the tunnel widened a bit. Large rocks jutted from the edges of the path as the space widened further.

A pained grunt echoing through the catacombs had me picking up the pace, my feet carrying deeper into the mountain. As soon as I rounded the last corner, though, I had to duck. A white orb of magic sailed past my face, exploding against the cave wall.

Rock and debris rained on me as I got knocked back,

my shoulder slamming into the opposite wall. Struggling to stand, I pushed forward. Two men faced off against each other—their magic raging as their blades clashed. A sweeping turn later and I realized I recognized them both—their faces far too familiar.

*Bishop La Roux and August Theodore Davenport III.*

Perfect.

## 21

Davenport spun his thin sword in an arc as he shot an orb of white magic at Bishop. The mage deflected the spell before it could land with power of his own, the ball of light exploding against the stone and rocking the entire cavern. A fissure cracked the rock, the concussion nearly blowing me off my feet.

Ears ringing, heart racing, I searched the tunnel behind me for J and Jimmy. Seeing no one, my heart slowed just a little. J was safe—for now.

But how far had I run, and how fast?

I whipped my gaze back to the battle before me. Bishop's arms were coated in his power, the black and purple swirls racing up his arm as a ball of magic formed in his palm. He, too, had a sword, only Bishop's was thicker, cruder, and made from the dark death magics he harnessed. The roiling blade was not of this world and just the sight of it made my stomach go into free fall. His sword reminded me of Tabitha's soul, the putrid, fetid thing that had crawled out of her body after I'd taken her life.

Bishop's weapon resembled a dark spirit, the awful buzzing of it clanging inside my head.

Davenport's sword swirled in the air, the blade moving almost faster than my gaze could track. But as fast as that blade was, Bishop managed to avoid it—at least for a little while. All too soon, that blade made contact with Bishop's flesh, slicing into the skin of his belly before raking across his cheek.

Bishop hunched over, cradling his stomach as Davenport stood over him with a ball of magic glowing in his hand.

"Did you really think I'd let you get away with it? Huh? That I wouldn't figure you out? You betrayed the wrong man, La Roux." Davenport reared his arm back, ready to let that orb fly.

But I couldn't let Davenport kill Bishop. It didn't matter that we were on the outs.

"Hey," I shouted, unable to think of anything better to say. But I didn't need to be witty to get the job done. My presence distracted Davenport for just a moment, his eyes wide, a touch of fear coloring his expression, allowing Bishop the upper hand.

Without so much as a word, Bishop gathered himself enough to slice his blade through the director's middle. As he stood, he ripped the sword up, spilling blood and viscera all over the dirt floor. Davenport's face paled as he staggered back. Sword forgotten, he clutched at his middle, disbelief warping his features.

Then the director crumpled to his knees, falling face-first onto the gritty ground.

For a second, I felt an overwhelming sense of relief. Davenport had tried to have me killed.

*Twice.*

He'd threatened my friends, my life, my job. He hated me—hated everything I was and everything I stood for.

And if it wasn't for the laugh coming out of Bishop's mouth, that relief probably would have stayed. I would have relished the short reprieve before finding my brother. But the more I watched Bishop, the less and less relief I felt.

Davenport's blood coated his hands, and oddly, Bishop gazed lovingly at the scarlet liquid. His laughter died, his irises glowing bright gold as his power rose on the air. Then the blood seemed to soak into his skin, feeding him in a way I had never seen before.

His gaze strayed to Davenport's shriveling body. As old as Davenport was, his remains would decompose quickly, rendering to ash before the hour was out. Bishop smiled as he watched his former boss start to decay into nothing.

"What are you doing just sitting there?" Davenport's ghost yelled, startling me out of my horror-filled reverie of my ex-boyfriend quickly losing his mind. "You got me killed, you idiot."

Shaking my head, I opened my mouth to deny it, but Davenport cut me off before I could speak.

"I don't give a shit about your excuses. Don't you know what you've done? I'm not the bad guy here," he insisted, waving at Bishop. "He is."

But it didn't make any sense.

Davenport had taken Essex to the black site instead of killing him.

Davenport had wanted me dead.

Davenport had tried to kill Bishop.

"Don't listen to him, Darby," Bishop growled, stalking over to me, his eyes glowing gold as swirls of black and purple magic raced up his arms. "He's lying to you."

The former director got in my face, causing me to rear back and smack my head against the stone wall.

"Can't you see he's lying? I'm *dead*. My work here is done. But you can still stop him."

I shook my head at them both, crab-walking backward to get away.

"You fucking idiot," Davenport growled. *"Fine.* If you can't figure it out, I'll just show you." The director raced in my direction, latching onto me with a determination I'd never seen from the dearly—or *not* so dearly—departed. His soul fell into my chest, filling my mind with the facts of his demise, what he'd seen, what he'd felt.

The slice of Bishop's blade ripped through my stomach as I experienced Davenport's death firsthand, his last thoughts racing through his mind as his final breath left him. But more, I saw the raid on the black site through his eyes, and the man flanked by wolves as he tore through the building agent by agent to free my brother, killing anyone in his path.

My eyes flashed open as Bishop yanked me from the ground, his power-soaked hands gripping my upper arms tight enough to bruise. Gold swirled in his irises, his face pleading as he shook me just a little too hard.

I wanted to keep my expression blank, but his betrayal—his deceit—made me physically ill.

"Why?" I choked, staring at a man I didn't seem to

know at all. "Why would you free him? After all he did, after all he took. Why?"

Bishop's grip tightened, those bruises a certainty now, but I barely felt it. Everything had been a lie. Everything. The truth of it hit me in the stomach and my gorge rose.

"I did it for us, Adler. For us." He shook his head, his smile just a touch wrong. "Davenport was going to find out everything Essex made me do for him. And it wasn't like I got all my sins wiped clean. That deal your sister made was for your immunity, not mine." His smile was bitter as he pressed his forehead against mine. "As soon as Essex told him what I did, I'd get thrown in jail or worse."

Fear clogged my throat, making me almost freeze. His words didn't make any sense.

*What kind of boiled bunny bullshit is this?*

"I thought you said you didn't know about my brother until Greyson." It was true that Essex was the Overseer of the ABI, but Bishop had sworn he hadn't made the connection between my brother's evil deeds until Agent Greyson had been murdered.

Bishop shook his head, pulling me tighter to his chest. "You don't understand."

Shoving him back, I took three steps away, trying to see his face. It was one thing to be an asshole to me and act like a child. It was a whole other to have lied to me from day one.

"Did you know the whole time?" I whispered, tears filling my eyes. I blinked them away, needing to see. "Tell me. Did you know Essex was my brother the whole time? Did he send you?"

"You don't understand," he insisted as he erratically whipped his head from left to right.

Rage ignited through my chest as the betrayal took root. "Did. You. Know?"

He began to pace, the blade reforming in his hand. "Of course I knew. I've been at Essex Drake's beck and call for centuries. But he didn't send me to you. Mariana did. As punishment." He tapped his forehead with the flat of the blade. *"Look but don't touch, mage,"* he said, mimicking Mariana's voice. *"We need her for this to work."*

Bishop's laugh sent a cold pit of dread down my spine, my breaths clogging in my lungs as I remembered what he'd said to me.

*There is not a rule I wouldn't break, a line I wouldn't cross for you...*

*I'd rain down Hell itself on this world to keep you...*

*I've killed people...*

"She didn't know what you mean to me. She couldn't see how fucking special you are. Neither of them could see it." He rushed me, backing me into the wall, taking advantage of my shock. "You have to see it. Can't you? That we're meant to be together. That we're meant to always be together."

*I am not a good man...*

*I've done things I knew were wrong...*

*I'd burn down the world...*

*No one has sacrificed anything for me...*

His hot breath skated over my skin, and I couldn't hide my shudder. Every line he'd thrown my way that seemed so special at the time now just sounded deranged. He'd told me exactly who he was, but I didn't believe him.

"Then why free Essex? Wh—"

"Always with the questions," he gritted out, grinding his teeth. "Don't you get it? If Essex never told him anything, then I could have my freedom. I just had to keep the powers that be from finding him for a while until I could get rid of Davenport. And would you look at that? I took care of it."

His magic rose high on the air as the purple swirls of power raced over his hands. "Now sit still. You don't believe me now, but you will. You always do."

The violet magic flowed over me, coating my body but not sticking as it slithered off my skin but never landing. This was exactly what he'd done on the porch, only now I understood.

Blood magic.

Bishop was half blood mage, and he was using that power on me. To change my mind? To make me believe him?

*You don't believe me now, but you will. You always do.*

Did that mean that everything I'd felt, every kiss, every hug, every laugh, was all a lie? He'd touched me, loved me, had sex with me...

I wanted to throw up. He might as well have roofied me.

"You took my will away," I whispered, a part of my heart—a part of my soul—shriveling up inside my chest and dying. "You stole it. You stole everything. Was any of it me? Did I choose any of it?"

Confused, he latched onto my arms, shaking me before slamming me into the rock wall. "Why isn't it working anymore?" he seethed through his teeth, spittle flying from the corners of his mouth. "That fucking demon did something to you, didn't he? He locked me out. I'll fucking kill him."

Aemon had prevented anyone from possessing me, not spelling me. But something I was wearing did. What had Jimmy said about the pendant?

*Think of this like a bulletproof vest.*

When had Bishop's behavior started?

When had Bishop's apologies stopped working?

When had I started to see him for what he really was?

When was the first fight we'd ever had?

Right after Jimmy clasped that chain around my neck.

Bishop's gaze drifted down to my collarbone, and he shook his head as he tried to focus on the pendant.

"What's this?" he growled, fisting his fingers over the chain and yanking for all he was worth.

The metal didn't so much as quiver. He wrenched his hand this way and that, but not only did the metal not cut into my skin, the clasp never budged once.

"*Is this it?*" he shouted in my face, crowding me against the stone. "That fucking Fae spelled you. Can't you see that? Can't you see they're trying to take you away from me?" He roughly pressed his forehead against mine as he pushed his body closer. "I told you. We're not done, Adler. Remember? We'll never be done."

Shaking, I slowly wrapped my hand over the hilt of my dagger, desperately trying to keep the disgust from my expression. I didn't want his touch on my skin or his breath in my face. I didn't want him anywhere near me. And I for damn sure was not his—not now.

Not ever again.

"Where is Essex, Bishop?" I asked softly, keeping every single emotion locked inside. "Tell me where he is, and then we can just be us, right? That's what you want, isn't it?"

The side of Bishop's mouth curled up in chagrin. "You don't mean that. You're lying." He punched the wall beside my head, his power cracking the stone as if it were plaster. "Stop lying to me."

Fighting off the urge to gag, I ran my nose against his, mingling our breaths together. "I'm not lying. Just tell me. I'll make sure he never tells a soul what you did. You won't have to worry about him ruining us ever again."

Bishop's smile was all teeth. "Did you know your blood races when you lie?" He reached between us to tap on the exact spot where Aemon had healed me. "I can feel it speeding through your veins—pumping so hard as you spin your web of bullshit."

My fingers tightened over the handle of the blade, and I yanked it free as I shoved him back. "Tell me where he is, Bishop."

"Why, Adler?" he taunted as black overtook the gold in his eyes. "You going to beat it out of me?"

"If I have to."

He clucked his tongue as he raised his arms, his power rising along with them. "I told you we weren't done. That we'd never be done, but I was wrong, wasn't

I? You're never going to listen to me. I'll always have to change your mind."

*Is this walking sack of shit complaining about having to spell me? Oh, the poor baby.*

"You know, I think you were right before," he said, his cracked rambling getting louder. "We really should break up."

Bishop brought his arms down in a swift sweep, the earth rocking in answer. Magic as dark as the depths of Tartarus itself wound around his arm, swirling up his neck. The wicked blade reformed in his hand as a vicious smile carved its way across his face.

"I might not be able to spell you, but I can still spell the dead. How do you feel about zombies, Adler? Because I gotta say, when it comes to ripping you apart? I fucking *love* them."

## 22

It made a sick sort of sense that I was running toward a horde of zombies instead of away from them. But the fact of the matter remained that my two closest friends were in between me and said zombies, and it didn't matter that Bishop deserved all my wrath.

J and Jimmy didn't deserve his.

As soon as that spell was cast, I did a little power throwing of my own, shoving Bishop La Roux into the closest wall hard enough to crack his fucking skull. Too bad it didn't stop what he'd started.

And hadn't Bishop warned Cassius about this very thing? That there were thousands of dead bodies in these mountains—remains of the unknown departed just moldering in the hills for him to scoop up and use as cannon fodder?

*He told you who he was all along. You should have believed him.*

Shuddering against that truth, I raced around another bend in the tunnel, hoping I got to my friends before Bishop's spell did. I quickly found out I was a smidgen too late.

The cloying odor of death clung to the air as Jimmy whipped his sword through the neck of a half-decomposed man, sending his body flying against the tunnel wall, sans head. His blade never stopped as it cut through corpse after corpse—some wolf, some not—but he was doing everything in his power to keep J safe.

J wasn't taking this shit lying down, either, as he lined up head shot after head shot, conserving his bullets until his aim would be true.

My power rose in my chest, spilling out of my hands in a wave of golden light, shoving the horde back.

"'Bout time you showed up," J huffed, expelling the spent mag from his Glock and reloading. He chambered a round and tipped his chin to his gun. "I don't think this is gonna cut it, do you?"

"No," I murmured as I shook my head, swallowing hard. My gaze strayed to the snapping wolves and clawing humans, their fight not dying an inch, even though they were momentarily blocked. Unless I stopped the mage who'd started the spell, there was nothing to do but mow through the dead and hope we didn't end up counting ourselves among them.

Jimmy's breath sawed in his lungs as he took a knee, his head resting on his viscera-covered sword. "What the fuck happened? It was as if you disappeared. One second you were there and then you took off. We ran after you, but you were too fast. Then all of a sudden these—I don't even know what they are—started attacking. They look like zombies, bu—"

"They are."

Both J and Jimmy stared at me as I focused on trying to keep the horde back.

"What death mage did you piss off now? There's no wa—"

Slowly, I shifted my focus to my best friend, allowing him to see the truth on my face. I'd known J and Jimmy most of my life. They knew every expression and every wound. I had no idea what my face told J, but he reared back, rage and fear and a fair amount of revulsion on his.

"No," he said in disbelief. "Not Bishop. I know you guys broke up, but I thought he was just an asshole not a murderer."

*But he told you he was a killer, didn't he? You just didn't know that he was a psychopath to boot.*

The ache in my chest that I was trying so desperately not to feel yawned wide enough to swallow me whole. "We'd both be wrong on that front." My gaze shot to Jimmy. "We need to kill him. It's the only way these things will stop."

That wasn't precisely true. I was sure if I managed to actually knock him out, they'd go bye-bye as well. But killing Bishop was a solid plan with real merit and it should be explored.

Posthaste.

Jimmy's gaze traveled to the pendant he'd clasped around my neck. "I should have given that to you sooner. I didn't know—"

"Stop it," I barked, directing my attention to the dead. "He fooled a lot of us. Now, about a plan?"

But neither Jimmy nor J got a chance to answer me. The earth beneath our feet rocked hard enough that I worried the whole tunnel would collapse on our heads. We had to move. Scrambling to avoid falling rocks, we raced ahead of the chasing horde. When J stumbled, I snatched his hand, hauling him behind me as we weaved through crushing stones and crumbling walls.

Soon we were back in the stupid fucking antechamber with Bishop, only this time he wasn't alone. More dead teemed behind him, seeming to just be waiting for us to show up.

*Fine.* He wanted to play it that way? I bent, letting go of J as I snatched a throwing knife from my boot. Without much in the way of aim, I let it fly as I prayed for someone somewhere in this great wide universe to throw me a fucking bone. The silver blade rotated end over end as it sailed across the wide cavern, embedding in Bishop's shoulder with a satisfying *thunk.*

Shock traversed his warped features. The blight of his death magics crawled up his neck and across his skin —the magic staining parts of his tan flesh with the darkness of the dead. Bishop's sneer was a thing of nightmares as he balled his fists, pumping more and more of his power into the mountain.

He didn't so much as look at the blade in his flesh or my friends. No, his hate, his attention, and his power were all directed at me. I pulled on what little unspent magic I had left, aiming it all at Bishop.

This time, however, I did not catch him by surprise. His crazed smile bloomed wider as a ball of shadow formed in his open hands.

"Say hi to your brother for me."

Before I could get a shot off, that orb of black death magics slammed into the ground right in front of me, blowing me off my feet and knocking me into the arms of the dead. Fingers clawed at my skin, my hair as I struggled to breathe, the crushing weight of the horde shoving me to my knees. Bones stabbed my flesh as I swung my dagger wide, my dying power not shoving them back an inch.

*Help me. Please, someone help me.*

I didn't know if I screamed those words or just thought them, but I wasn't going to make it out of here —the reality of this fact weighing down my limbs.

A flash of white caught my eye, and I hacked through the dead. At first, I thought it was Essex, his hallmark white hair a beacon for my rage. With a scream of pure hate, I shoved a rotting wolf back, ready to track down my brother. But when I charged, it wasn't Essex.

It was Sloane.

Her worried expression filtered through the throng, and in my surprise, I was caught in the crowd once more. A putrid bite from a red wolf broke my stare, and I slashed, taking its head before I charged forward again, only to be pulled back.

*She came for me. This must mean that I'm... I'm...*

*I'm not going to make it, am I?*

Her smile was small, sad, before she disappeared in the crowd of teeming dead bodies. No offense to my little sister, but if I was going to die in the middle of a zombie horde, I'd rather she just got on with it.

She was the new Angel of Death, couldn't she just yank me out of my body, no muss, no fuss?

A searing stab to my gut burned through my body, and I stuttered to a stop, staring at the bony hand embedded in my flesh. A decaying human skeleton snapped its jaw in my face—teeth gone, flesh hanging in long strips from its bones.

My breath caught in my lungs, and I stumbled to my knees.

This was it.

This was where I ended.

Then a flaming ax cut through the dead, knocking their corpses away from me. Darkness swarmed me, almost like smoke but solid, too, shoving through the throng. Hell, for a second, I thought I was hallucinating until a hand wrapped around my back and yanked me from the depths.

The smoke was dense as it curled around me, protecting me from teeth and talons and claws—its ax slashing through Bishop's spell as if it were no more than tissue paper.

"You are a handful, you know that?" Aemon's voice floated on the air, burrowing its way into my ear. For some reason, the Prince of Hell seemed rather put out that I was in the middle of this mess. Honestly, I couldn't blame him. This situation was a solid ten on my bullshit scale.

The smoke's grip tightened as we spun, avoiding a falling boulder.

"Honestly, you need a keeper."

Confused, I stared at the smoke, squinting until I found familiar fiery eyes and twisted horns. I'd only seen them the once—and only for just a moment—but their memory was burned in my brain.

*Oh, now I get it. Aemon is the smoke. The smoke is Aemon. Aemon the smoke man.*

"Hello, Aemon." I giggled, loopy for some reason. Darkness clouded my vision, and I seriously doubted it was him. If I had a guess, it was most likely the blood loss. "You see my sister around here anywhere? I think she's here for me."

The smoke held me tighter as my head lolled back. I knew it was trivial, but I didn't want to die in a place like this. I wanted the sun on my face one more time or maybe the moon. I wanted to feel clean again, wanted to say goodbye to everyone. It wouldn't be so bad, would it?

"Can't say I have," he growled, testy for some reason. "Then again, she'll need to go through me first if she wants you."

We spun again, the world twirling as we moved through the tunnel.

"She'd win, you know. She's strong. And she doesn't like it when people tell her what to do."

The smoke pulled back, reforming into the shape of Aemon's pretty face, his blue eyes glittering in the torchlight. "It's a family trait then?"

Snorting, my head lolled again as the darkness got thicker around the edges of my sight. "Probably right."

"It was the boyfriend, right?" Aemon growled, pulling me tighter into his chest. "He did this to you?"

"Not my boyfriend anymore," I murmured sleepily, not sure why I needed to make that distinction.

I was dying, for fuck's sake.

Who gave a shit whether Bishop La Roux was my boyfriend or not? He was a flaming sack of dog shit with the moral compass of a frat guy's nut sack. No, that wasn't right. The frat guy's testicles were probably a better specimen of decency than he was.

And I was just one on a long list of people he'd killed, or helped kill, or stood idly by and let die. The last in line of people he'd spelled, he'd hurt, he'd lied to.

"Good to know," Aemon murmured, sitting me down on the cool ground. With the burning ache in my middle, the cold felt nice. "But you aren't dying, remember?"

That just showed how much he knew. I didn't have

anything left to heal with—no more energy, no more souls. And I was tired.

And when had I told him I was dying?

A finger ran over my forehead to my nose, skating over my lips to my neck and then down to the center of my chest. "Remember how much it hurt the first time? This will be easier."

"Wh—"

My question was cut off by a scream, the searing agony of his healing burning through me like gasoline on a brush fire. And again, like a strike of lightning, it was gone.

Aemon's mouth pulled into a smug grin as he phased into his hellish form. "I told you. You aren't dying on me. Now stay put while I go find your ex. I'll even let you kill him. Make it good, will you?"

Then he was gone.

The smoke that seemed to protect me dissipated with him as it revealed the hellscape that was left of the tunnels. Boulders jutted from the ground in almost every direction, the cavern half-collapsed in some places. Zombies still littered the space, but most of them lay in heaps on the dirt.

Glittering gold magic mixed with the silver of a sword sliced through a dwindling group, a wolf baiting Jimmy as if he just wanted to play. I found my feet, racing to help Jimmy. Granted, I only had a single dagger left and two throwing knives, but it was something.

But where was J?

My best friend ducked under Jimmy's arm, bashing in the head of a wolf with a chunk of limestone as it lunged for his boyfriend's side. There wasn't exactly a smile on his face, but he wasn't screaming for the hills, either.

I was almost to him when a wolf snaked around the arc of Jimmy's sword and lunged for J. The skeletal jowls latched onto J's neck, clamping down on the tender flesh. The beast jerked—ripping, tearing before its decaying eyes rolled back in their sockets, then its jaw loosened, and the thing fell to the dirt.

My scream seemed to shake the earth off its axis as golden power leaked from me, slamming into the remaining horde with enough rage and pain to rip a hole in the world. I caught J as he fell, his scared eyes searching for mine as he tried to say something.

Now I knew what Sloane was here for—or rather, *who*. Shaking, I brushed the dark hair off his forehead as I pressed my other hand to the wound at his neck, trying to stop the flow. I'd already done this once, hadn't I? Watched as a member of my family withered in my arms?

Well, I couldn't do it twice.

My hand tightened on his wound, and I shoved with my power. I'd done it so many times before—healing those with what little I had left. With my father, he had been too far gone to heal, but J?

I didn't care what deal I had to make, what line I had to cross. He was staying here. So I shoved and pushed, the tell-tale trickle of a nosebleed not stopping me one bit.

"You're gonna be fine, Cooper. You hear me? You're gonna be fine," I insisted, wilting into him as what was left of me attempted to put Humpty Dumpty back together again.

But there just wasn't enough for the both of us.

That was okay. It was okay. He could have it. He could have it all.

"Jimmy's gonna take care of you," I promised, hoping that wasn't a lie. "You're gonna grow old together, okay? You're going to be happy." I pressed a trembling kiss to his forehead and heaved, my body going floaty, my sight dimming. "Love you," I whispered. "So much." My breath stuttered as I struggled to give him the rest. Just a little more and he'd make it. I was sure of it.

A hand closed around my arm, yanking me away from my best friend.

*No. He's going to make it. I can't do this again. Please, just let me save him.*

Clawing for J didn't do any good, whoever had a hold on me was so much stronger than my will. In their hold, I wilted, trying to crawl for my best friend.

*You can't have him, Sloane. You hear me. You can't have him. Take me. Take me instead.*

Ironclad hands held me in place as Hildy's voice pierced through my brain, the world completely dark. "For fuck's sake, lass. You're too far gone. Eyes bleeding, barely breathing. What were you thinking?" He paused, his words pitched low. "Can you help her? The vampires are a little busy with Cooper. Please. I'll make a deal if need be."

I didn't need help. I needed to get to Jeremiah. But my struggles and cries fell on deaf ears.

"No deal needed, grave talker," Aemon answered, his voice getting farther and farther away even though his hold stayed firm. "I told her she wasn't dying today, and I won't be made a liar."

So it was Aemon's fault I couldn't get to J.

"Is he going to make it?" Aemon murmured, his voice barely a whisper.

"Only time will tell."

## 23

I reared back as a plate of spaghetti was shoved in my face, nearly knocking me over.

"For the love of fuck, just eat something," Ingrid growled, pressing the plate right under my nose. Considering all I smelled was zombie guts, nothing was appetizing—especially spaghetti.

We were on day three of me waiting for J to wake up from his turning, and I wasn't moving until I saw some sign of life from him. I hadn't eaten, hadn't showered, and I for damn sure hadn't left his side since waking up in an unfamiliar house. This room could have been made of cheese for all I noticed.

My gaze hadn't shifted more than an inch from my best friend's face in three days. Not when Sarina had given me her spiel, not when Deimos showed up to call me off looking for his son—which was the only good thing to come out of my interruptions. The only time I'd moved was when Sloane came to visit. I'd screamed my head off at my sister when she'd shown up, warding her off as best I could.

She couldn't have him. She'd just have to take me instead. And I wasn't taking my eyes off him until he woke up, just in case she came back.

I didn't need sleep. I needed Björn's weird hybrid vampire mojo to fucking well work. It wasn't until after the process of J's turning had been started, did I learn that Ingrid could never make a vampire—her small stature preventing her from completing the task.

Björn was the only one left to turn J, but there were enough complications to that mess that I stopped listening after a while. Evidently, the big man was only half-vamp, warlock blood taking up the other half. And he'd never turned anyone before—his half-breed status making the process a little iffy.

"Don't make me call your demon, Darby. I'll have him put you to sleep again, so help me. Then I'll dunk your ass in soap until you stop smelling like death."

For a moment, my glare shifted to my small friend, not bothering to give her a response. Aemon was currently second on my shit list, the bastard Prince of Hell sealing J's fate when he yanked me from him. At the top was Bishop, his death on my schedule just as soon as J got his shit in gear and opened his eyes.

The man in question was clean and dry, the wound at his neck healed. According to Ingrid, the process usually took a single day—not three—and I feared my friend might never wake up.

"Give it a rest," Jimmy croaked from his perch on the bed beside J. "You don't hear me bitching about it."

Sarina picked her head up from the floor, her short hair just as much of a mess as I figured mine was. "Me either."

The oracle met my gaze for a moment before quickly sliding it away, shame staining her face. I hadn't been the only one Bishop had spelled, and the implications of her time near him had her questioning everything she thought she knew about herself and her powers. Or at least that's what she'd said as she continued to apologize for all she'd missed.

There was only so many times I could let her tell me sorry before I lost it, so I stopped listening to her, too. She'd been the one to suggest the necklace, so in a way she'd been the one to set us both free.

"Or me," Dave muttered, his face covered in a hat as he lounged in a hard-backed chair in the corner, his legs stretched out and ankles crossed. Except for me, he'd slept the least, constantly taking calls from the pack about recovery efforts in the catacombs. There were a lot of people missing or dead—the collapse of the tunnels nearly taking out entire families. He wouldn't be able to stay much longer, his new pack getting restless without their leader.

"That's because you're all nose blind from being near her so long. She's making the baby vamps gag in the basement, you guys. The *basement*."

And I'd had enough. "Then put a fucking air purifier in here or clear out the house. I don't give a fuck what you do, but I'm not moving until he wakes up, Ingrid. I'm not going to say it again."

It didn't matter that I barely had enough strength to keep my eyes open, I would fight her if need be.

Just as soon as I was able to stand.

"Please tell me this isn't Hell," J croaked, covering his eyes with his arm and making me almost fall off my perch on the cedar chest.

Jimmy lunged for him, wrapping the smaller man up in a hug so tight I thought J might burst. J returned it, ducking his head against Jimmy's chest. The action was probably not smart, given that J was now an apex predator, but I just couldn't give a shit.

"Why is it so loud?" he said, the words muffled by Jimmy's chest. "Why is the room so bright? And for the love of god, what is that smell?"

Relief had me nearly passing out, my whole body wilting so fast, Ingrid had to hold me up.

"Well, I got some good news and some bad news, sport," she replied. "Which one do you want first?"

Lifting his head, J stared at Ingrid with his regular old blue eyes. "Bad. Always the bad first."

"Your life as you knew it is over," she announced matter-of-factly. "Good news? You actually have a life to live."

J sat up *fast-fast*—too fast—scaring himself by the way his face paled, his eyes flashing red for just a moment.

"Aww, man. Am I a vampire now?" His fingers found his mouth, running over his distinctly not-vampire fangs. Typically vamps had needlelike fangs that descended or retracted over their regular blunted teeth. Like Björn, J's fangs were just extensions of his canines —far prettier, if less functional.

Ingrid shrugged, jostling me in the process. "We'll get into the details later, for now, maybe tell your bestie to take a shower please? She's bugging the world."

Sorrow lined his face as he met my gaze. I hadn't wanted this for him, and he hadn't wanted this for himself. And I didn't know if he would accept the new life that had been shoved into his lap.

"Go take a shower and fucking eat something. Then get some sleep."

I wanted to—I really did—but making sure he was okay was more important.

"Please?" Then he gave me a patented J smile. "If you do it—without question—I'll forget the DK incident."

DK stood for Dewey Kincade, my first crush who'd made me laugh while I was eating crackers, and I'd accidentally spat them all over his arm. To date, it had gone down in history as my most embarrassing moment. Any time I ate cheese crackers, J would bring it up and I'd relive the shame.

"Done."

He was still J, and I was still me, and things would go back to normal—or normal for us. And when he was ready, he and I would find Bishop La Roux and make him pay for what he'd done.

I moved, and the scent of my shirt wafted up, making me gag.

Okay, shower first.

Rinsing my hair of its third shampoo, I seriously contemplated shaving my head. The smell of death lingered around me, and it wasn't my clothes. As soon as I undressed, Ingrid stole them, telling me she'd toss them in an incinerator somewhere.

*Fair enough.*

"Now that J is out of the woods, are you going to listen to me now?" a voice called in the bathroom, and I nearly busted my ass on the stone tile as I slipped in soap suds.

"Sloane?" I called, wiping shampoo out of my eyes. "What the fuck?" I fought off the urge to cover my bits, even though she couldn't see me through the frosted glass.

"I'm trying to give you good news, you stubborn ass, and you keep shooing me away," she grumped. "So now that you know J isn't going anywhere, are you going to stay put and listen?"

Considering I was in the shower, naked, I kind of had no other choice. "Sure thing, Sloane. I'm all ears."

My sister grumbled loud enough that I heard her over the spray. Something about me being a massive pain in her ass.

"I'm not going to get into that bullshit you pulled in the cave—which was peak stupidity, by the way—but you need to know. I was never here for J, or you, you little shit. I was in that tunnel for our brother."

Getting up on my tiptoes, I peeked over the shower door, meeting Sloane's purple gaze. "What?"

Arms crossed over her chest, booted foot cocked to the side, my little sister raised a single eyebrow at me. "Yep. Our brother is in Tartarus where he belongs. Unfortunately, your ex did the honors, but I can't exactly complain."

I'd been doing my level best to *not* think about Bishop La Roux—not until J's fate had been secured. Her bringing him up now had me lowering back to my heels and shoving myself under the spray.

"You're sure?" I asked, my voice pitched low, but she'd still hear me.

She let out a bitter bark of laughter. "Since I took him to Tartarus myself? I'm sure."

Funny, I hadn't spent much time thinking about Essex, but the relief of knowing he was gone had my legs buckling underneath me. Planting my ass on the tile, I tilted my head until it was under the water.

What had Bishop said?

*Say hi to your brother for me.*

No wonder he didn't tell me where Essex was—the fucker had killed him already.

A lump swelled in my throat as the weight of the last week crashed over me. I was glad Essex was dead— ecstatic even—but having to be thankful to Bishop for ending his life? That was something I just couldn't bear.

Sobs ripped up my throat—the relief, the fear, the revulsion all mixing together.

The water turned off, and slender arms wrapped around me as I cried. "It's okay, Darby. You're going to get him. And if you don't, I will."

Snorting through my tears, I said, "I thought you couldn't tell me shit. What about Fate?"

She brushed the wet hair out of my eyes, pulling my chin up to meet her gaze. "This is your freebie pass. I'm flipping off Fate for you, just this once."

Giving her a tremulous smile, I nodded, my nerves easing just a bit. If there was one thing Bishop La Roux couldn't escape from, it was Death herself.

Two days later, I was back at the Warden house, pouring myself a cup of coffee. After J woke up and his life changed, I had to go back to mine, and it required coffee. I poured Tobin a cup and passed it to him.

"You find anything?" I asked, chewing my lip.

Tobin shook his head, sipping the brew as he slid a file my way. On top of our Nero research—which was still ongoing—our new mission was finding Bishop. I'd given up on looking for Aemon after Deimos' mysterious decree, and I wasn't complaining. He'd said something like "you've trapped him and don't even know it," or some other such nonsense.

Granted, at the time, I wasn't paying too much attention. The god would pop up soon enough, demanding as ever, asking for something else. I just knew it.

Opening the file, I scanned the scant information, my irritation growing. Other than the ABI files—that they refused to divulge, the fucks—Bishop La Roux was a ghost. No properties. No bank accounts. Not a fucking thing to track his ass down, and it was pissing me off. I was close to calling Sloane in on her offer to find him, but if she was going to flip Fate off for me, I wanted to make sure it was worth it.

The debriefing with the council was a doozy—especially when I got to tell snooty Lise Dubois what her grandson had been up to with Essex Drake. The expression on her face when she learned just how deep he'd been in my brother's web was priceless. Sure, Davenport wasn't a huge loss, but the intel that man had... well, it was enough to sink Bishop's whole life.

*What he had of it.*

The ABI was in complete shambles, and the council was considering shutting down the Knoxville branch permanently, letting the arcaners police themselves for once. My Warden job was secure—for now—and I'd been getting backup as soon as Björn said that J was safe to be in public.

The doorbell rang, and either Yazzie or Acker yelled that they were answering it.

Somehow all of us had made it out of the catacombs relatively unscathed, my guys aiding the council members with aplomb. Tobin had even gotten a commendation after saving Kato's ass, his shotgun skills on point.

After everything, I wasn't too keen on visitors, and even less likely to answer the door. That didn't stop every wolf matriarch and patriarch stopping by to drop off food or a gift or whatever. Dave hadn't been shy informing the wolves who they owed for removing their former leader. I didn't agree, but being the alpha of his own pack, Dave didn't have to listen to me.

Much.

"Darby?" Yazzie called and I looked up, waiting for him to continue. When he didn't, I silently shoved back from the island, shooting Tobin the universal gesture for "shut the fuck up."

Picking my way through the house back to the front door, I had one hand resting on the gun at my spine and the other on the hilt of a brand-new dagger. I didn't go anywhere anymore without either—even to sleep— doing my best to be ready when and if a certain someone came calling. I wasn't sure if I'd ever really sleep again—not with Bishop out there somewhere. And it didn't matter if the wards had been changed or that I was always armed, the knowledge I had would be burned in my brain forever.

Which was why when I spied Yazzie and three women in the foyer—two I knew and one I didn't—I narrowed my eyes.

"They said they know you. Were rather insistent that I let them in," he explained, answering my scorching glare.

At my continued censuring silence, he shrugged.

He was conned by a couple of pretty faces and all I got was a shrug? *Oh, we were going to have a talk about this.*

"What? They smell like Ingrid," he muttered before escaping the foyer in favor of safety elsewhere.

Rolling my eyes, I greeted my guests. "Dahlia, Harper. Nice to see you again. Who's your friend?"

Dahlia St. James and Harper Jones were members of the Night Watch and were my sister's closest friends. Dahlia opened her arms for a hug, but I held up a hand. People touching me would be off-limits for a while. Hell, maybe forever. Frowning, she stepped back as Harper gave me a finger wave.

I'd never have to worry about hugs from Harper, the empath reluctant on casual touches.

The third lady seemed familiar, though. But since her face was mostly covered in oversized glasses, I couldn't tell. The woman in question lowered her shades, her dark gaze far more recognizable than a legally dead woman's should be.

Shiloh St. James shot me a grin as she snapped her fingers. Instantly, a jewel at her wrist began to glow as a spell activated, changing her features before my eyes. Her body shrunk two inches as her nose got longer, sharper. Then her hair shortened to a bob as it bled from black to auburn.

"Now that that's out of the way," she said airily, waving her hand, "good to see you, doll. How's tricks?"

The former leader of the now-defunct Knoxville coven wouldn't breeze into town unless it was absolutely necessary. And two witches and an empath at my front door at five in the afternoon on a Tuesday?

*Yeah, nothing suspicious about that.*

I raised my eyebrow in the universal signal to "cut the shit." Emotions and pleasantries were no longer in my wheelhouse.

"Fine. You got a problem, darling, and I hauled my ass all the way from Georgia to help you out." She brushed a lock of now-auburn hair off her cheek.

She's been "dead" for less than a month, and now

she was in Knoxville potentially blowing her cover? This had to be good.

"Tell me," she said, "what do you know about a vampire named Nero?"

*Darby's story will continue with*
**Dead Wrong**
*Grave Talker Book Six*

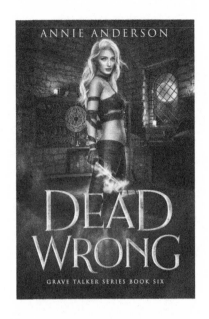

**DEAD WRONG**

*Grave Talker Book Six*

**Never make a deal with a demon.**

There are two things Darby Adler wants more than anything: to take a vacation, and to find who is responsible for the rash of witch abductions in Knoxville.

With an ancient vampire in town and a slew of fugitives on the loose, her suspect pool is vast. But Darby has a sneaking suspicion she knows the culprit all too well.

And if she can't catch him on her own, she might just have to resort to more *creative* measures to get the job done.

Here's hoping she doesn't lose her soul in the process.

***Preorder on Amazon today!***
*Coming May 10, 2022*

**SPELLS AND SLIP-UPS**

*The Wrong Witch Book One*

**I suck at witchcraft.**

Coming from a long line of famous witches, I should be
at the top of the heap. Problem is, if there is a spell cast
anywhere in my vicinity, I will somehow mess it up.

As a probationary agent with the Arcane Bureau of
Investigation, I have two choices: I can limp along and
*maybe* pass myself off as a competent agent, or I can
fail. *Miserably.*

Worse news? If I can't get my act together, I may not only be out of a job, I could also lose my life.

*Whose idea was this again?*

***Preorder now!***
*Coming June 7, 2022*

*Want to get to know Darby's sister? Check out...*

## NIGHT WATCH

*Soul Reader Book One*

*Waking up at the foot of your own grave is no picnic... especially when you can't remember how you got there.*

There are only two things Sloane knows for certain: how to kill bad guys, and that something awful turned her into a monster. With a price on her head and nowhere to run, choosing between a job and a bed or certain death sort of seems like a no-brainer.

*If only there wasn't that silly rule about not killing people...*

*Grab Night Watch today!*

# THE PHOENIX RISING SERIES

*an adult paranormal romance series by Annie Anderson*

Heaven, Hell, and everything in between. Fall into the realm of Phoenixes and Wraiths who guard the gates of the beyond. That is, if they can survive that long...

*Living forever isn't all it's cracked up to be.*

**Check out the Phoenix Rising Series today!**

EXCLUSIVE SNEAK PEEKS,
GIVEAWAYS, BOOK DISCUSSION.
COME FOR THE BOOKS.
STAY FOR THE MEMES.

To stay up to date on all things Annie Anderson, get exclusive access to ARCs and giveaways, and be a member of a fun, positive, drama-free space, join The Legion!

# ABOUT THE AUTHOR

 Annie Anderson is the author of the international bestselling Rogue Ethereal series. A United States Air Force veteran, Annie pens fast-paced Urban Fantasy novels filled with strong, snarky heroines and a boatload of magic. When she takes a break from writing, she can be found binge-watching The Magicians, flirting with her husband, wrangling children, or bribing her cantankerous dogs to go on a walk.

To find out more about Annie and her books, visit www.annieande.com